"I'm not money crazy,"

Teddi said proudly. She jerked her hand out of King's grasp, and this time he let her go. "I have everything I need."

"Do you really?" he retorted. "Then why do you live with your aunt—why does she have to keep you?"

"Think what you like," she told him. "You will anyway."

King looked down at her quietly. "Does it bother you?"

She shrugged carelessly. "You don't really know anything about me."

His eyes dropped to her soft, full mouth. "I know that underneath that perfect bone structure and bristling pride, you burn with sweet fires when you want a man to kiss you...."

Dear Reader,

There are a few very special romance writers whose books always become "keepers," and Diana Palmer is *definitely* one of those all-time favorite authors. So, for Diana's loyal fans—and for those who have just discovered this award-winning, bestselling author—we are delighted to announce the return of her much-loved Silhouette Romance novel, *Darling Enemy*.

Emotional and compelling, *Darling Enemy* celebrates the positive values, the belief in love and commitment, the intense passion, that keep readers coming back to Silhouette Romance novels time and time again.

"Fashion a Whole New You" also enables us to bring you three other Silhouette books that have not been available recently: *Sarah's Child* by Linda Howard, a Silhouette Special Edition, *Bachelor Father* by Annette Broadrick, a Silhouette Desire, and *A Very Special Favor* by Kristin James, a Silhouette Intimate Moments. All four of the "Fashion a Whole New You" selections are love stories that I know will capture your heart.

At Silhouette Books, we strive to bring you the very best in romance reading... from our heart to yours!

Valerie Susan Hayward
Senior Editor

Diana Palmer

DARLING ENEMY

Silhouette Romance®

Published by Silhouette Books New York
America's Publisher of Contemporary Romance

To Amilee, who taught me how to believe in myself

SILHOUETTE BOOKS
300 E. 42nd St., New York, N.Y. 10017

DARLING ENEMY © 1983 by Diana Palmer
Originally published as a Silhouette Romance.

FASHION A WHOLE NEW YOU edition
published in September 1991.

ISBN: 0-373-15161-6

DIANA PALMER

has written over forty novels for Silhouette Books. A five-time winner of the Waldenbooks Bestseller Award, this acclaimed Silhouette author first got her start writing as a newspaper reporter. Diana Palmer debuted in the Silhouette Desire line, and her first Silhouette Romance novel—*Darling Enemy*—was published in 1983. In California's *Affaire de Coeur*, she was listed as one of the top ten romance authors in the country.

Watch for the next LONG, TALL TEXAN—*Evan*—from Silhouette Romance in September!

Silhouette Romance
DARLING ENEMY by Diana Palmer
Teddi Whitehall knew that rancher King Devereaux
was convinced she was nothing but a glamorous
playgirl. She also knew the truth wasn't going to
change his mind. So why did she feel so alive when
he was near?

Silhouette Desire
BACHELOR FATHER by Annette Broadrick
Tony Antonelli had broken Susan McCormick's
heart ten years ago, and every day their son was a
constant reminder of their shared night of passion.
Now Tony was back. Could two hearts ever mend
and beat as one again?

Silhouette Special Edition
SARAH'S CHILD by Linda Howard
Sarah had loved Rome Matthews for so long that
becoming his wife had made her world almost
complete. Only having his baby could have made her
happier. But Rome couldn't risk losing another
child—though the decision might cost him the
woman he loved....

Silhouette Intimate Moments
A VERY SPECIAL FAVOR by Kristin James
Adam Marshall's good deed for the month was to
initiate Emily, his shy secretary, into womanhood.
But when the wallflower became a perfect rose, his
cool detachment fled, and he began to lose his heart.

Chapter One

It was the most glorious kind of morning, and Teddi Whitehall leaned dreamily on the windowsill of the dormitory room overlooking the courtyard below, watching the pigeons waddle like old men over the cobblestones.

The buildings on college campus were romantically Gothic, like something out of another century. But its green and flowering grounds were what Teddi liked most. They were a welcome change from the sophisticated New York apartment where she had to spend her holidays.

She leaned her face on her crossed arms with a sigh and drank in the smells and sounds of the early morning. She dreaded the time when she'd have to board the plane back to New York, away from the ex-

clusive Connecticut college and her friend and roommate Jenna. There was a chill in the June air, and the
beige gown that complemented Teddi's short dark hair
and huge brown eyes was hardly proof against it. It
was a good thing that Jenna had already gone downstairs, she thought, and couldn't chide her about her
impulsiveness in throwing open the window.

Jenna wasn't impulsive. In that, she was like her
older brother. Teddi shivered delicately. Just the
thought of Kingston Devereaux was enough to cause
that reaction. They'd clashed from the very beginning. The big rancher with his Australian drawl and
cutting smile might have sent the other girls in the
dormitory into swoons, but he only made Teddi want
to turn away. He'd made his contempt for her more
than evident during the years she'd been friends with
his sister. And it was all because of a false impression
he had, which nothing she said could change. His snap
judgments were as unfair as his treatment of Teddi,
and she dreaded visits to the Canadian ranch with
Jenna. Teddi had an uncomfortable feeling that Jenna
was getting ready to spring another invitation on her,
since they were both free until fall quarter began.
Kingston Devereaux would fly his plane over from
Calgary to get Jenna, and Teddi would find excuses to
avoid him . . . as usual.

She shook her head miserably. At least Jenna had a
mother and brother to go home to. Teddi had no one.
Her aunt, who was her only living relative, was somewhere on the Riviera with her latest lover. The New

York apartment Teddi shared with her on holidays was going to be particularly empty now. At least there would be plenty of modeling offers forthcoming, she was assured of that. She'd been modeling since her fifteenth birthday. She was blessed with good bone structure and eyes so large and poignant that one of her boyfriends had likened them to a doe's. The modeling agency that handled her was proud of its star client—if they had a complaint, it was that she was being wasted in the halls of academia.

She felt suddenly chilled to the bone and drew back into the room, closing the window with nervous hands. Modeling was the sore spot with Kingston, who had the immutable opinion that models and virtue didn't mix. It hadn't helped that Teddi's aunt was notorious for her affairs. Kingston was an old-fashioned man with narrow-minded views on modern permissiveness. He might have an affair himself, but he had nothing but contempt for women who indulged. And he was certain Teddi did.

She'd never forgotten her introduction to him. She'd met Jenna at boarding school when she was just fifteen, and the two girls had become fast friends. She'd expected Jenna's family to be equally friendly and caring, and had received the shock of her young life when Kingston Devereaux had shown up at Christmas to fly Jenna home to the ranch outside Calgary for the holidays.

His first reaction to Teddi had been strangely hostile, a long, lingering appraisal that had touched Teddi like a cold finger against her bare skin. Jenna's gay announcement that she'd invited Teddi for the holidays had been met with a cold, gray glare and a reluctant acceptance that had spoiled the trip for her. She'd done everything but move outside to keep out of the big man's way. Then, and since.

She shook off the memories along with her gown, and slipped into a silky beige pantsuit that her aunt had mailed to her for Easter—one of a number of presents that were supposed to take the place of love and affection. Teddi ran a comb through her short, thick hair and decided against makeup. Her complexion was naturally olive, her lips had a color all their own, and her long-lashed eyes never needed enhancing. She slipped into a pair of low-heeled shoes and went downstairs to find Jenna, idly wondering why her roommate had rushed out in the first place.

She started into the dormitory lounge and stopped, frozen, in the doorway. Jenna was sitting stiffly on the couch, facing a big, elegantly dressed man with gold-streaked blond hair.

"...And I said no," Kingston Devereaux stated flatly, his back to the doorway, his Australian accent thick. "She's not going to turn my damned cattle station upside down again the way she did at Easter. Can you see the men getting any work done? Hell, they do nothing but stare at her."

"She won't cause any trouble," Jenna retorted in defense of her friend, venom in her normally sweet tone. Her gray eyes, so much like Kingston's, were flashing with anger. "King, she's nothing like her aunt, she's not what you think . . . !"

"Too right, baby, she isn't rich, and she's never going to be, unless she can get her claws into some poor, trusting male." He rammed his big hands into the pockets of his slacks, stretching the expensive gray fabric across his flat stomach, his powerful, broad thighs. "Well, she isn't going to spend the summer making cow's eyes at my men—or at me," he added with a bitter laugh.

Teddi, listening, blushed. That Easter vacation had haunted her.

"King!" Jenna gasped. "You must know that Teddi's frightened of you, you've made sure of it. She'd never . . ."

"Wouldn't she?" he growled. "Surely you noticed the way she stared at me during Easter? An Easter I'd have preferred spending alone with my family," he added with a cruel smile. "Mother should have had another daughter to keep you company, then maybe you wouldn't spend your life picking up strays!"

Teddi's face went white. She stood there like a wounded little animal, her huge eyes misty with the hurt, and Kingston turned at that moment and saw her. The expression on his broad, hard face was almost comical.

"Oh, Teddi," Jenna wailed, grimacing as she, too, caught sight of her and realized that her friend had heard every harsh word of the conversation.

Teddi straightened proudly. "Hello, Jenna," she said softly. "I—I just wondered if you wanted to have breakfast with me. I'll be at the dining hall."

"King came early," Jenna said helplessly, with a shrug. "We were talking about vacation."

"You'll enjoy yours, I'm sure," Teddi said, forcing a smile to her full, faintly pouting lips. "I'll go ahead..."

"I want you to come to the ranch for the summer," Jenna said with a defiant glance at Kingston.

"No, thanks," Teddi said quietly.

"King won't even be there part of the time," the smaller girl said sharply, tossing her long, pale-blond hair.

Teddi glanced at the taciturn rancher, whose jaw was clenched taut. "I've spent quite enough of my holidays being treated like an invading disease," she said deliberately. "I'd rather spend this one alone, and I'm sure your brother will be delighted to have his family to himself," she added venomously.

"Teddi—" Jenna began.

"I've got modeling assignments lined up, anyway," Teddi added truthfully with a last, killing glare at Kingston as she turned. "Why spend my vacation on a ranch when I can seduce half the men in New York while I make my fortune?" Her lower lip was trembling, but no one could see it now. "Thanks anyway, Jenna, thanks a lot. You can't help it that you've got an insufferable snob for a brother!"

And on that defiant note, she stormed out of the dormitory into the sunshine, her back rigid, the tears welling up in her smoldering eyes.

She walked over the cobblestones numbly, the tears coming in hot abundance, trickling down into her mouth. How could he be so cruel, how could he? The conceited ass! As if any woman would be stupid enough to get herself emotionally involved with that arrogant Australian...the gall of him to accuse her of making cow's eyes at him! She flushed at the memory. He'd never let her live down her foolish behavior at Easter; if only she'd realized that he was teasing....

She fished in her pocket for a tissue. As usual, there wasn't one. She brushed the back of her hand angrily across her cheeks, hating her own weakness. She'd write to Jenna, he couldn't stop her from doing that, and they'd be together when the fall quarter started. Kingston couldn't keep them from being friends, after all. He'd never had a chance once they'd enrolled at the same college.

She passed a couple of her classmates and tried to smile a greeting just as a lean, commanding hand caught her arm and jerked her around, marching her to the shade of a nearby oak.

"Running again?" Kingston Devereaux asked curtly, his glittering eyes biting into hers. "You've done a lot of that."

"Self-preservation, Mr. Devereaux," she replied coldly, brushing wildly at one stray tear. "You make me forget that I'm a lady."

"A lady?" he drawled. "You?" His eyes ran down her slender body, over the high young breasts and down the tiny waist and sweetly curving hips to her long, graceful legs in their clinging cover.

"Oh, excuse me—in your exalted opinion, that's a title I don't deserve," she replied coolly.

"Too right," he ground out. He lifted his broad shoulders restlessly. "Jenna's back at the dormitory crying her damned eyes out," he added roughly. "I didn't come all this way to upset her."

"Upsetting people is one of your greatest talents," Teddi told him, glaring back.

One eyebrow went up as he studied her face. "Careful, tiger," he drawled. "I bite back."

Teddi wrapped her arms around herself, turning her attention to passing students. "You've done nothing but attack me for the past five years," she reminded him. "And for your information, Mr. Devereaux," she added hotly, "if I stared, it was out of apprehension, wondering what minute you were going to start something!"

"You started it the last time, darling," he reminded her, smiling coldly at the blush she couldn't prevent. "Didn't you?"

She didn't like being reminded of that fiasco, and her eyes told him so. She turned away.

"How long did it take you to perfect that pose of innocence?" he asked.

"Oh, years," she assured him. "I started while a baby."

He looked down his arrogant nose at her. The sunlight made gold streaks in his dark-blond hair. "You didn't get to your particular rung on the modeling ladder without giving out a little, honey. You'll never convince me otherwise."

"Why bother to try?" she countered. "You're so fond of the playgirl image you've foisted on me. And you're never wrong, are you?"

"Not often," he agreed. "And never about women," he added, with just a trace of sensuality in his deep drawl.

She supposed that he'd had his share of women. Her own small experience of him had been devastating. He had an eye-catching physique and when he liked, he could be charming. Teddi, having seen him stripped to the waist more than once, couldn't find a fault in him. A picture of his bronzed, hair-roughened muscles danced in front of her eyes, and she shook her head to get that disturbing memory out of her mind. Kingston disturbed her physically, he always had, and she disliked the sensations as much as she disliked him. He was the enemy, she mustn't ever lose sight of that fact.

"You know very little about the type of modeling I do," she said numbly.

"More than you think," he corrected. "We have a mutual acquaintance."

She let that enigmatic remark fly right over her head as she started walking.

"Going somewhere?" he challenged.

"To inflict myself on someone else over breakfast," she agreed cheerfully. "Strangely enough, there are people who don't think of me as a walking, talking 8 × 10 glossy photograph."

"Fair dinkum?" he murmured, falling into step beside her.

She glared at him. "Believe what you like about me, I don't care." But of course she cared, she always had. She'd gone out of her way to try to make Kingston like her, to earn even the smallest word of praise from him. But she'd never accomplished that, and she never would.

"You can have breakfast with Jenna and me," he said after a minute, as if the words choked him. They probably had, she thought miserably.

"No, thanks," she said politely. "I can't eat wondering if you've had time to sprinkle arsenic over my bacon and eggs."

A chuckle came out of his throat, a surprising sound. "You never stop fighting me, do you?"

She shifted her shoulders lightly. "I've spent most of my life fighting."

"Poor little orphan," he murmured coldly.

She glared at him. "I loved my parents," she said curtly. "Shame on you for that."

He had the grace to look uncomfortable, but only for an instant. "Hitting below the belt?" he asked with a lifted eyebrow.

"Just exactly that."

"I'll pull my punches next time," he assured her.

"You make it sound like a game," she grumbled.

"Oh, no, it's stopped being that," he replied, his eyes on the dining hall ahead. "It stopped being that at Easter."

She colored delicately, her eyes closing for an instant to try to blot out the memory. She hated him for reminding her of what had almost happened.

"I should have taken you right there in that stall instead of pushing you away," he said in a husky, deep whisper.

She moved jerkily away from him. "Please don't remind me of the fool I was," she said tightly, avoiding his glittering eyes. "I had you mixed up with someone else in my mind," she added to salvage what she could of her pride.

His features seemed to harden even more. "And we both know who, don't we, honey?"

She didn't understand, but was too angry to ask questions. "If you're quite through, I'm hungry."

His darkening eyes traced her face, the slender lines of her body, as if the word triggered a hunger of his own.

He moved closer and she stiffened, catching the amused, curious glances of the other students on their

way to and from the dining hall. "People are staring," she murmured nervously.

"Afraid they'll think we're lovers, honey?" he
asked with magnificent insolence.

She reacted without thinking, her fingers flashing
up toward his hard, tanned cheek. But he caught her
wrist just in time to avoid the blow, holding it firm in
a steely, warm grip.

"Temper, temper," he chided, as if the flash of fury
amused him. "Think of the gossip it would cause."

"As if you'd ever worry about what people thought
of you," she returned hotly. "It must be nice to have
enough wealth and power to be above caring."

He searched her dark, dark eyes for a long time.
"Your parents were poor, weren't they?" he asked in
an uncommonly quiet tone.

She flushed violently. "I loved them," she muttered. "It didn't matter."

"You push yourself way too hard for a girl your
age," he said. "Who are you trying to show, Teddi?
What are you trying to prove? Jenna says you're
studying for a major in English—what good is that
going to do you as a model?"

She tugged at his imprisoning hand. "None at all,"
she admitted, grinding the words out, "but it'll be
great when I start teaching."

"Teaching?" He stood very still, staring down at
her as if he doubted the evidence of his own ears.
"You?"

"Please let me go..." she asked curtly, giving up the unequal struggle.

His fingers abruptly entwined with hers, the simple action knocking every small protest, even speech, out of her mind as he drew her along the cobblestoned path beside him. She wondered at her own uncharacteristic meekness as the unfamiliar contact made music in her blood.

"You'll come home with us," he said quietly. "The last thing you need is to be alone in that damned apartment while your dizzy aunt bedhops across Europe, with no one about to look after you."

She knew he disliked her Aunt Dilly, he'd made no secret of the fact. She'd often thought that his dislike for her aunt had extended automatically to herself, even though she was nothing like her father's sister.

"You don't have to pretend that you care what happens to me," she said coldly. "You've already made it quite clear that you don't."

His fingers tightened. "You weren't meant to hear that," he said. He glanced down at her. "I say a hell of a lot of things to Jenna to keep the issue clouded."

She blinked up at him. "I don't understand," she murmured.

He returned her searching look with a smoldering fire deep in his gray eyes that made her feel trembly. His jaw tautened. "You never have," he ground out. "You're too damned afraid of me to try."

"I'm not afraid of you!" she said, eyes flashing.

"You are," he corrected. "Because I'd want it all, or nothing, and you know that, don't you?"

She felt her knees going weak as she stared up at him, the words only half making sense in her whirling mind. One of Teddi's friends walked past, grinning at the big, handsome man holding Teddi's hand, and King grinned back. Women loved him, their eyes openly interested, covetous. But the looks they were attracting embarrassed Teddi, and she tried to pull loose.

"Don't," King murmured, tightening his warm fingers with a wicked smile. "Don't read anything into it, it's simple self-preservation. If I hold your little hand, you can't slap me with it," he added with a chuckle.

It was one of the few times she'd ever heard him laugh when they were together, and she studied his lofty face, fascinated. She was of above average height, but King towered over her. He wasn't only tall, he was broad—like a football player.

"Like what you see?" he challenged.

"I was just thinking how big they grow them in Australia," she hedged.

"I'm Australian born," he agreed. "And you're from Georgia, aren't you? I love that accent . . . early plantation?"

She pouted. "I have a very nice accent; nothing like that long, twanging drawl of yours," she countered.

"A souvenir from Queensland," he agreed without rancor.

She searched his eyes. "You spent a lot of your life there," she recalled.

He nodded. "Mother was a Canadian. When she inherited the Calgary farm, we left Australia and moved to Canada. That was before Jenna was born. Dad and I spent a lot of time traveling between the two properties, so mother and I were little more than strangers when I was younger."

"You don't let anyone get close, do you?"

He stopped at the door of the dining hall and looked down at her. "How close do you want to get, honey—within grabbing distance of my wallet?" he asked with a cold smile.

She glared up at him. "I'm not money crazy," she said proudly. She jerked her hand out of his grasp, and this time he let it go. "I have everything I need."

"Do you really?" he retorted. "Then why do you live with your aunt—why does she have to keep you?"

She wanted to tell him that she made quite enough modeling to pay her school fees and to support herself. But she hadn't seen the sense in trying to maintain an apartment of her own when she was in school nine months out of the year. Besides, she thought bitterly, Dilly was rarely at the New York apartment these days. There was always a man....

"Think what you like," she told him. "You will, anyway."

He looked down at her quietly. "Does it bother you?"

She shrugged carelessly. "You don't really know anything about me."

His eyes dropped to her soft, full mouth. "I know that underneath that perfect bone structure and bristling pride, you burn with sweet fires when you want a man to kiss you...."

Her face flamed. She moved away as he opened the door for her, standing in such a way that she had to brush against his powerful body to enter the dining hall. She glanced up at him as she eased past, her eyes telling him reluctantly how much the contact disturbed her.

"Soft little thing, aren't you?" he asked in a deep, lazy drawl, his eyes pointedly on the high thrust of her breasts as they flattened slightly against his broad chest in passing.

Teddi was grateful that Jenna was already at a table waiting for them, so that she didn't witness the strange little scene. Jenna tended to carry teasing to an embarrassing degree.

Chapter Two

Breakfast was pleasant. It was one of the few times Teddi could remember sitting down to eat with King when he didn't go out of his way to needle her. She had the strangest impression that their fiery relationship had undergone a change while they talked earlier. She looked into his eyes and blushed, and the reaction caused an amused glint in his own eyes.

"How soon can you girls get packed?" King asked over a final cup of coffee. At a nearby table, several female students were openly watching King with every bite, their eyes dreamy.

"I'm taking a flight to New York later this afternoon," Teddi said quickly.

King watched her, reading accurately the panic in her young face. "You and I will iron out our differences this summer," he said in a tone that made her tingle all over. "In the meantime, there's no excuse for denying Jenna your company just to spite me."

It was the truth, but part of her was afraid of what settling those differences might lead to. She was nervous of men in any physical sense, and especially of King—there were scars on her emotions that she didn't want reopened.

"I've got modeling jobs—" she began.

"You can live without them for a few weeks, surely?" he taunted. "Twenty-four-hour days are only bearable for short terms," he reminded her. "You've been holding down a night job, Jenna told me, in addition to your day courses. Quite a feat, if I remember curfew regulations."

"The gates close at midnight here," Teddi murmured. She glared at Jenna, who managed to look completely innocent.

"All the same, you could use a vacation. As long as you don't spend it mooning over me," he added.

Her eyes jerked up to find him smiling in a teasing way, his eyes kind and glittering with good humor. It surprised her into smiling back, accentuating her beauty to such a degree that King just sat and stared at her until she dropped her own gaze, embarrassed.

"Besides," King added tautly, "where else have you got to go? With that nymphomaniac of an aunt, or to an apartment alone?"

"A half hour ago, you wouldn't have cared if I'd had to shack up with a bear at the local zoo," she reminded him hotly.

He cocked an eyebrow. "As I recall, Miss Cover Girl," he murmured, "the subject of bears once got us into an interesting situation."

She went fiery red, avoiding Jenna's smiling, curious gaze. "An *un*bearable situation," she murmured, laughing when King got the pun and threw back his own head.

"Please come," Jenna added, pleading. "If you're around to chaperone me, King will let me chase Blakely all over the ranch," she laughed.

"Blakely?" King frowned. "You don't, surely, mean my livestock foreman?"

Jenna peeked at him through her lashes. "I'm interested in ranching," she murmured.

"Don't get too interested in Blakely," he warned. "I've got bigger plans for you."

"Do you always try to run people's lives?" Teddi challenged.

He looked deep into her eyes. "Look out, honey, I might fancy running yours if you aren't careful."

"I'm hardly worth notice," she reminded him. "An orphan with no connections, a background of poverty, a sordid reputation..."

"Oh, hell, shut up," he growled, getting to his feet. "I've got to have the plane serviced. You two get packed."

He stormed off. Jenna giggled openly, her eyes speculative.

"Just what is going on?" she asked Teddi. "I've never seen him off balance like that."

"I have been practicing sorcery," Teddi said in a menacing whisper. "While he wasn't looking, I slipped a potion in his coffee. Any second now, your tall, blond brother is going to turn into a short, fat frog."

Jenna burst out laughing, tears rolling down her cheeks. "Oh, I can't wait to see him," she laughed. "King, with green warts!"

Teddi laughed, too, at the absurdity of fastidious King with such an affliction. He never seemed to have a hair out of place, even when he was working with the livestock.

Hours later, they were well on the way to Calgary in King's private Piper Navajo.

"I can't wait for you to meet Blakely," Jenna told her friend. "King just hired him a couple of months ago and I got to know him when I was home for that long weekend in April."

"He must be something special," Teddi murmured.

Jenna sighed. "Oh, he is. Brown eyes and red hair and a build like a movie star. Teddi, you'll love him…but not too much, please," she added, only half teasing. "I couldn't begin to compete with you, as far as looks go."

"Don't be silly," Teddi chided. "You're lovely."

"You're a liar, but I love you just the same," came the laughing reply. Jenna leaned back in the plush seat. "King didn't chew you up too badly, did he?" she asked after a minute. Her gray eyes met Teddi's apologetically. "I could have gone through the floor when he made that nasty remark and I saw you standing in the doorway and knew you'd heard."

"King and I have been enemies for years," Teddi reminded her friend, her dark eyes wistful. "I don't know what I did to make him dislike me so, but he always has."

"It puzzles me," Jenna murmured, "that King gets along so well with everyone else. He has that arrogant streak, of course, but he's a pussycat most of the time. He's worked twenty-two-hour days to keep us solvent since Dad died. Without him the whole property would have gone down the drain." She eyed her friend. "None of which explains his hostility toward you. I couldn't believe my eyes when he went out of the dormitory after you."

"That makes two of us. I very nearly hit him."

"How exciting! What did he do?"

Teddi reddened. She was not about to admit that King had held her hand all the way to the dormitory. "He ducked," she lied.

Jenna laughed delightedly. "Just imagine, your trying to plant one on my brother. Do you know, you never used to stand up to him. When we were younger, he'd say something hurtful and you'd go off and cry, and King would go out and chew up one or two of his

men.'' She laughed. ''It got to be almost funny. The
men would start getting nervous the minute you
walked onto the property.''

Teddi shifted restlessly. ''I know. To be honest, I've
been turning down your invitations lately to avoid
him. I probably wouldn't have gone home with you at
Easter if I hadn't been trying to shake off that friend
of Dilly's who's been pursuing me.''

''Would you mind very much telling me what happened at Easter?''

''I threw a feed bucket at him,'' Teddi blurted out.

Jenna's eyes opened wide. ''You're kidding!''

Teddi's gaze dropped to her lap. ''It was just a mild
disagreement,'' she lied. ''Oh, look!'' she exclaimed
as she looked out the window. ''We must be over Alberta, look at the plains!''

Jenna peeked over her friend's shoulder and looked
down through the thick cloud cover. ''Could be,'' she
murmured, checking her watch, ''but we haven't been
in the air quite long enough. I bet it was Saskatchewan.'' She got up. ''I'll ask King.''

Teddi's eyes followed the smaller girl while her mind
went lazily back to the spring day when King had
chided her about her private life just one time too
many....

Jenna had slept late that morning, but the bright
sun and the sounds of activity out at the stables had
roused Teddi from a sound sleep. She'd put on her
riding outfit and hurried down to get Happy to saddle a horse for her. Happy, one of the older hands on

the huge Canadian ranch, had been one of her staunchest allies. He'd taught her to ride when King had refused to.

But Happy hadn't been in the neat stables that morning. King had. And the minute she saw him, she knew there was going to be trouble. He had a way of cocking his head to one side when he was angry that warned of storms brewing in his big body, a narrowing of one eye that meant he was holding himself on a tight rein. Teddi had been too angry herself to notice the warning signs.

"I know how to ride," she argued. "Happy taught me."

"I don't give a damn," he growled back. "The men have seen bear tracks around this spring. You don't ride alone on the ranch, is that clear?"

She felt an unreasonable hatred of him, raw because he hadn't even noticed her painfully shy flirting, her extra attention to her appearance. She had been trying to catch his eye for the first time in their turbulent acquaintance and it hadn't worked. Her temper had exploded.

"I'm not afraid of bears!" she all but screamed.

"Well, you should be," he replied tightly, his eyes roaming over her. "You don't know what a bear could do to that perfect young body."

The words had shocked her. Amazingly, now that she had his attention, she was frightened.

She backed away from him, and that had caused a quaking kind of anger to charge up in his big body.

"Afraid?" he chided. "You probably know more about sex than I do, so why pretend? Just how many men have had you?"

That had been the final straw. There was a feed bucket at her elbow, and she grabbed it without thinking, intending to fling it directly at him.

He hadn't kept his hard-muscled body in shape by being careless. He stepped out of the way gracefully and before she had time to be shocked at her own behavior, he stepped forward and caught her by the wrists, roughly putting her hands behind her and pinning her against him.

"That," he growled, "was stupid. What were you trying to prove, that you don't like what you are?"

"You don't know what I am!" she cried, wounded. Her huge brown eyes had looked up at him with apprehension.

"No?" His big hands had propelled her forward until her soft, high breasts were crushed against the front of his blue-patterned cotton shirt. She smelled the fresh, laundered scent of it mingling with his cologne. It was the closest she'd ever been to him.

"You've behaved like a homeless kitten around me lately," he said in a deep, sensuous tone that aroused new sensations in Teddi's taut body. "Low-cut blouses, clinging dresses, making eyes at me every time I turn around...." He released her wrists then, and his calloused hands eased under the hem of her blouse, finding her bare back. They lingered on her silky skin, faintly abrasive, surprisingly gentle. "Come closer, little one,'' he murmured, watching her with calculating eyes, although she'd been too lost in his darkening gaze to notice that.

Her legs had trembled against the unfamiliar hardness of his, her breasts had tingled from a contact that burned even through the layers of fabric that separated her from his broad, hair-covered chest.

His hands were causing wild tremors all over her body as he savored the satin flesh of her back and urged her slender hips against his.

''I want your mouth, Teddi,'' he whispered huskily, bending, so that his smoky breath caressed her trembling lips. ''And you want mine, don't you, love? You've wanted it for days, years...you've been aware of me since the day we met.'' His mouth had hovered over hers tantalizingly while his hands caressed her back, made mincemeat of her pride, her self-control. ''You want to feel my hands touching you, don't you, Teddi?'' he taunted, moving his head close, so that his mouth brushed tormentingly against hers when he spoke.

''King,'' she moaned, going on tiptoe to try to catch his poised, teasing mouth with her own.

He'd drawn back enough to deny her the kiss, while his hands slid insolently down over her buttocks and back up again. ''Do you want me to kiss you, Teddi?'' he'd asked with a mocking smile.

''Yes,'' she whispered achingly, ''yes, please...!'' Anything, she would have agreed to anything to make him kiss her, to bring the dream of years to reality, to let her know the touch and taste and aching pleasure of his hard, beautiful mouth.

"How much do you want it?" he persisted, bending to bite softly, tenderly at her mouth, catching her upper lip delicately between both of his in a caress that was blatantly arousing. "Do you ache, baby?"

"Yes," she moaned, her eyes slitted, her body liquid under his as her knees threatened to fold under her. "King, please," she half-sobbed, "oh, please!"

He lifted his head, then, to study her hungry face and a look of pain had come over his features. He turned away so that she never saw whether he had to struggle to bring himself under control. She doubted it. Certainly there was no sign of emotion on his face when he turned back to her.

"Maybe for your birthday," he said with magnificent arrogance. "Or Christmas. But not now, honey, I'm a busy man."

He gave a curt laugh and she stood there like the ruins of a house—empty and alone. Her eyes had accused, hated, in the seconds that they held his.

"You're not human," she choked. "You're as cold as . . ."

"Only with women who leave me that way," he interrupted. "My God, you'd even give in to a man you profess to hate, you need it so much!"

She watched him walk away with her pride around her knees. She'd sworn to herself that day that she would toss herself over a cliff before she gave him the chance to humble her again. She avoided him successfully for the rest of the Easter vacation, and when she boarded the plane for Connecticut with Jenna, she hadn't even looked at him.

She sighed, watching the clouds drift by outside the window. In her mind she relived that humiliation over and over again. She wondered sometimes if she'd ever be able to forget. The incident had revived other, older memories that had been the original cause of her frigid reaction to most men. Ironically, King had been the only one to ever get so close to her, to arouse such a damning response. And he didn't even know that to Teddi, most men were poison.

"Saskatchewan," Jenna said smugly, returning to reseat herself beside her friend. "But Western Saskatchewan, so it won't be too much longer before we get home." She gave Teddi a searching appraisal.

"Looking for hidden beauty?" Teddi teased.

"Actually, I asked King about that bucket you threw at him," she replied hesitantly.

Teddi's heart dipped wildly. "And?" she prompted, trying desperately for normalcy.

"I guess I should have kept my mouth shut," Jenna said with a sigh, turning toward the window. "Honestly, sometimes I think he lies awake nights thinking up new words to shock me with."

Teddi felt a shiver as she folded her hands in her lap and closed her eyes. Apparently King didn't want to be reminded any more than she did. It was just as well, King had made it perfectly clear that he despised her.

The Devereaux livestock farm, Gray Stag, was located in a green valley in the foothills of the Rocky Mountains, not far from Calgary. It had its own private landing strip and all the creature comforts any family would ever want.

The house itself was a copy of a French château, big and sprawling with a long, winding driveway and tall firs all around it. Fields of wildflowers bloomed profusely against the majestic background of the snow-capped Rockies. There was a tennis court, a heated swimming pool, and formal gardens which were the pride of the family's aging gardener. It always reminded Teddi of pictures she'd seen of rural France.

King taxied the plane toward the hangar, where a white Mercedes was parked. A petite, white-haired woman in a fashionable gray suit waved as they climbed out of the plane and onto the apron.

"Mama!" Jenna cried. She ran into the woman's outstretched arms, leaving King and Teddi to follow.

"My God, you'd think she'd been away for two years instead of two months," King growled.

Teddi glanced up at his set face, so deeply tanned and masculine that her fingers itched to touch it. She averted her eyes.

"It would be nice to have a mother to run to," she said in a tone that ached with memories.

She felt a lean, rough hand at the nape of her neck, grasping it gently in a gesture that was strangely compassionate.

"You haven't had a lot of love in your young life, have you?" he asked quietly. "It's something Jenna never lacked, we made sure of that."

"It shows," she agreed, watching her friend's warm, open smile. "She's very much an extrovert."

"My exact opposite." His eyes narrowed on the vista beyond the airport. "I don't care for most people."

"Especially me," she murmured.

His dark gray eyes pinned her. "Don't put words into my mouth. You know very little about me. You've never come close enough to find out anything."

She couldn't hold that dark gaze. "I did once," she reminded him bitterly.

"Yes, I know," he replied. His eyes sketched her profile narrowly. "I left scars, didn't I?"

She shifted her thin shoulders uncomfortably, wishing she'd never said anything in the first place. "Everyone's entitled to be foolish once or twice."

"I've wondered a lot since then what might have happened if I'd laid down with you in that soft hay," he said quietly, deliberately slowing his pace as they approached the rest of his family.

Her heart pounded erratically. "I'd have fought you," she said, her tone soft and challenging.

He looked down at her and a strange smile turned up his chiseled mouth at one corner. "Would you?" he asked in a deep, silky voice. "Do you have enough experience to know what it does to a man when a desirable woman fights him?"

"You seem to think I've slept with half the men in New York, so you tell me," she shot back.

He cocked an eyebrow. "I don't know what to think about you," he admitted. "Just when I'm sure I've got you figured out, you throw me another curve. I'm beginning to think I need to take a much closer look at you, Teddi bear."

She glared up at him. "Don't call me that."

"Don't you like it?" he taunted. "You're small and soft and cuddly."

She blushed like a teenager, and hated her helpless reaction to his teasing. It was just like before. All he wanted was to make her crawl. Well, he wasn't going to do it this trip.

"Don't think you'll ever get to cuddle me," she said shortly.

"And I wouldn't bet on that, if I were you." He pulled a cigarette from his shirt pocket and lit it while he watched her. "You were begging me for it in the barn that morning."

She shivered at the memory of her weakness and her eyes closed briefly. "You know a lot," she countered.

"What did you expect, that I spent all my time with the cattle?" he taunted. "I know what to do with a woman, young Teddi, as you damned near found out. I can lose my head, if I'm tempted enough. You brought that about, and we both know it. Those eye-catching little glances, those low-cut dresses, those come-and-kiss-me looks you were giving me—"

"I can't possibly tell you how sorry I am about the whole thing," she ground out. "Could we please just forget it? You're safe from me this trip, I wouldn't flirt with you if my life depended on it."

"That might be better," he murmured dryly. "I live in constant fear of being seduced by one of you wild city girls."

Now that did sound like flirting, but before she could be sure, they were within earshot of the others.

"The end of the world must be near," Mary Devereaux laughed. "Are my eyes going bad, or are you two actually not arguing for once?" She eyed her son closely. "And did I actually see you smile at her?"

King cocked an eyebrow at her. "Muscle spasm," he replied without cracking a smile.

"Sure," Mary laughed. She reached out and hugged Teddi affectionately. "It's so good to have you here, Teddi. What with King away most of the time, and Jenna's sudden interest in ranch management," she added with a pointed glance at her daughter, "I've been looking forward to a very lonely summer." She stared at the young girl. "Teddi, you aren't suddenly going to develop an interest in ranch management, are you?"

Teddi burst out laughing. "Oh, no, I don't think so."

"Thank goodness," Mary sighed. "Shall we go? I could use a cup of coffee. King, I suppose you'll drive?"

"When was the last time I let you drive me any-where?" he mused, leading the way to the car.

"Let me think." His parent frowned. "You were six and I had to take you to the dentist when you got into it with little Sammy Blain . . ."

Teddi hid a smile. She linked her arm with Jenna's and brought up the rear. It was nice to be part of a family, even for a little while.

Chapter Three

Teddi's room overlooked the Rockies. It was done in blue and white, with lacy eyelet curtains at the windows and a canopied bed. This was where she always slept when she came to Gray Stag—her own little corner of the old château.

She wondered who had occupied the matching room in the original home in Burgundy. One of King's ancestors had copied the design of his wife's family home to keep that grieving lady from getting attacks of homesickness when they'd settled in Calgary. The original château dated to the eighteenth century. This one was barely a hundred years old, but it had a charm all its own.

She opened the window and breathed the flower-scented air. Everything seemed so much cleaner in

Canada, so much bigger. Despite King's hostility, it
was nice to be here again. Mary and Jenna more than
made up for King.

Her eyes went to the soft bed. King. She remembered a night she'd spent at Gray Stag when she was
seventeen, during summer vacation.

She'd been fairly terrified of King back then, nervous and uncertain when he came near with his cruel
taunts. She'd never understood his dislike—she'd done
nothing to him to provoke it.

But that night there was a thunderstorm, violent as
only mountain thunderstorms can be. Teddi's parents
had gone down in a commercial airliner on a night like
this, and in her young mind she still connected disaster with violent storms. She was crying, soft little
whimpers that shouldn't have been audible above the
raging thunder.

But King had suddenly opened the door and come
in, still fully dressed from helping work cattle in the
flash flooding. His shirt was damp, carelessly unbuttoned to reveal a mat of hair and bronzed muscle that
had drawn Teddi's eyes like a magnet.

He eased down onto the bed and took the frightened, weeping girl into his big arms. He murmured
soft, comforting words that she didn't understand
while he cradled her against his warm, damp body, his
heart beating heavily under the cheek that lay on his
broad chest. He held her until the tears and the thunder passed, and then he laid her back down on the
pillows with a strangely tender smile.

"Okay, now?" he asked softly.

"Yes, thank you," she replied uneasily.

He stood there, looking down at her with strange dark eyes while she stared back, her eyes fixed on the sight he made, his shirt unbuttoned to the waist . . . it was the first time she'd been alone with a man in her bedroom at that hour of the morning, and her fear must have shown. Because he suddenly turned away with a muffled curse and was gone. After that night, he was even colder, and she worked even harder at avoiding him. Something had happened while they stared at each other so intensely. She still wasn't sure what it had been, but she remembered vividly the sensations she felt when his eyes had dropped to the uncovered bodice of her gown and traced deliberately every soft line of her young breasts under the half-transparent material. The memory was like a drawn sword between them, along with all King's imagined grievances against her.

There was a sharp knock at the door and Jenna peeked her head around it. "Come down and have something to eat," she said. "Mother's carving up a ham."

"Isn't Miss Peake here anymore?" Teddi asked as she joined her friend, remembering warmly Miss Peake's little kindnesses over the years.

"Our saintly housekeeper is visiting her sister for a few days." Jenna grinned. "She'd just die if she was here to see the size of the slices mother's getting off that ham. Mother eats like a bird, you know. Poor King!''

Teddi smiled involuntarily. "There's a lot of him to feed," she agreed.

"He gets even," Jenna assured her. "When mother's back is turned, he'll go in the kitchen and make himself a sandwich or two. He doesn't starve."

"Miss Peake was forever carrying him trays of food when he worked in the study," Teddi recalled, remembering how she'd strained for glimpses of him through that door at night.

"And he was forever complaining that there wasn't enough of it," Jenna added. "My brother has a tremendous appetite. For food, at least. Mother wants to see him married so badly, but he hardly ever takes anyone out. You'd think he doesn't know what to do with a woman, the way he avoids them."

Oh, Jenna, if you only knew, Teddi thought silently, as she remembered her own voice pleading for the touch of King's poised, taunting mouth. He knew far too much about women for a monk. Even Teddi, as inexperienced as she was, realized that.

But she didn't try to tell Jenna. It might lead to some embarrassing questions.

Teddi felt her pulse jump as they started into the spacious dining room, but if she'd hoped to find King there, she was doomed to disappointment. Only Mary was at the table, with cups of steaming coffee already poured and three places set.

"There you are." She smiled as the two girls joined her. "Isn't it a delightfully lazy day? I hope you're hungry, I've put on ham and bread and a nice salad for us."

Teddi had to muffle a giggle. There were enough pieces of bread for one sandwich apiece, and hardly enough ham to go around. And the nice salad would provide each of them with about two tablespoons. From her earliest acquaintance with Jenna, Teddi had been amused by Mary's eating habits. The fragile little woman had an appetite to match her stature, much to the chagrin of the rest of the family, and there was a good deal of moaning out of Mary's earshot. None of them would ever have said anything to hurt her feelings, but they couldn't resist a little good-natured joking among themselves.

"Don't tell me King's gone again?" Jenna asked as she and Teddi sat down, one on either side of Mary.

"Yes," Mary sighed. "To see about some kind of audit on that corporation of his in Montana. The board of directors retained an auditing firm from New York to do it."

Teddi didn't like to hear auditors mentioned. Some of her most unpleasant memories were due to one of her aunt's lovers, who was a very well-paid member of an illustrious New York firm.

"Is he going to be gone long?" Jenna wondered.

Mary shrugged. "A day or so, he said. But it's just the beginning. He may have to bring the dreadful man here as well—you know, to check the rest of the books." She caught the look on Jenna's face and laughed. "Yes, I know, this is Canada, but King reinvests some of the profits from the Montana operation into the livestock operation here, and..." She shook her head. "It's all very confusing. Ask King to explain it to you someday, I have no head for business management."

"Blakely does," Jenna murmured with a wry glance at her mother. "I could ask him."

Mary smiled at her. "I like Blakely very much. If you need an ally, my darling, you have one in me."

"Thanks, Mom," the young blonde said with a beaming smile. "It will take two of us to get around King."

"Get around King?" Mary paused with her fork in midair and stared at her daughter. "Now, Jenna..."

"Everything will be all right, I promise," came the smug reply. "Let's hurry and eat, Teddi, I want to introduce you to Blakely. You'll adore him!"

Blakely would have been adorable only to a girl who was in love with him, but he was personable and seemed to know his business. Teddi had to smother a grin at the worshipful look in Jenna's normally sensible eyes as they followed the thin, dark-eyed man around the property while the two young women were briefed on its operation. Blakely had red hair, so bright that it seemed coppery in the sun, and Teddi couldn't help but wonder what kind of children Jenna and the livestock foreman would have—blond ones or redheads. It wasn't going to be an easy thing if they were serious about each other. Jenna would never make King believe that it was she Blakely was interested in, not the millions she stood to inherit.

King. If only she could stop thinking about him! In view of his contempt for her, she should have detested him in return. But she didn't. She couldn't stop her eyes from following him whenever he was near. She felt an attraction toward him that nothing ever daunted, and she was helpless to prevent it.

She shook herself out of her troubled thoughts as Blakely mumbled something about the growth of the livestock farm.

"Originally," he informed the girls, "farms in Western Canada were laid out in 65-hectare parcels. And most of the farms are scattered within a 320-kilometer strip along Canada's southern border. But these days only about 5 percent of the work force is employed in agriculture," he added sadly. "Although productivity is increasing among those who remain, and mechanization has aided us quite a lot. Did you know," he continued, blossoming as he elaborated on his favorite subject, "that the average output of one farm worker today provides food for over fifty people?"

"I'd give that man a raise," Teddi murmured.

Blakely stared at her until the words penetrated, then he threw back his head and laughed, delighted at the little joke.

"Forgive me," he told her, "I do tend to get carried away about farming. I love it, you see. Not just the land, or working it and working with cattle on it; but the history and heritage behind it all. This was once part of the Northwest Territories," he said, sweeping his arms around to indicate the lush green valley in its summer splendor, with the tall, sharp peaks of the Rockies in the distance. "Alberta and Saskatchewan were organized out of it in 1905, but French fur traders were here long before then settling the wilderness. It's an exciting history, the settling of this territory, one I never tire of reading about. Or," he added sheepishly, "talking about."

"I like to talk about my part of the world, too," Teddi told him, "and I like learning about yours just as much. Please don't apologize. Think of it as cultural exchange," she added impishly.

"Thank you, Teddi," he replied with a smile.

"And now that we've got that settled," Jenna added, linking arms with the tall man, "let's see the rest of it."

Teddi followed along behind them, her eyes sweeping over the well-kept barn and stables, the white fences that kept the animals in, the huge fields of grain growing to feed the animals through the winter. It was an imposing sight. No wonder King loved it so. The scenery alone was lovely.

The next morning, Teddi went riding with Jenna and Blakely, keeping to herself, and eventually riding back alone to the ranch. It wasn't kind to tag along after them when they were so obviously falling in love and wanted to be alone.

She gave the horse to the ranch hand at the stables and walked aimlessly toward the house. Mary had driven into Calgary to shop, and there was no one to talk to. She didn't mind being alone here, though. It wasn't like being alone in that spotless New York high-rise apartment with the doors bolted and chained for safety. Here, there was help within earshot all the time. She'd never felt afraid at Gray Stag—mainly because it was King's domain, and she was afraid of nothing when King was around.

She walked into the house, idly wondering how much longer he'd be away. She was about to start up the stairs when King suddenly came down them, startling her.

He was wearing work clothes; a blue-patterned shirt open at the throat over worn jeans and dusty boots, and a straw Western hat jammed down over his blond hair at an arrogant angle.

"Where are they?" he asked without preamble.

"Your mother's gone shopping," she said uneasily.

"And Jenna?" he prodded, narrow-eyed.

She averted her gaze. "She's, uh, out riding."

"With Blakely?"

She glared at him. "What's wrong with Blakely?"

Both eyebrows went up. "Did I say anything was?"

She shifted, running her hand along the highly polished banister. "Well, no," she admitted reluctantly.

"You're always ready to expect the worst of me, aren't you?" he asked as he reached her, his eyes darkening as they slid over her face. She couldn't have imagined the picture she made, with her short, dark hair framing her face, her brown eyes like crystal, her cheeks just faintly flushed. "Your mouth is as red as a cardinal's breast."

She searched his quiet eyes, stunned at the compliment, something she'd never expected from King. King—her enemy.

He moved down another step, easing her back against the bannister with the threat of his big body. He reached down and cupped her chin with a lean, strong hand. His thumb stroked her lower lip lightly.

"How old are you now?" he asked in a deep, taut voice.

She swallowed. He was too close, too disturbing, far too masculine. He smelled of the outdoors, of a woodsy cologne and cigarettes. "I'm twenty," she said unsteadily. "I'll be twenty-one in four months."

"Too young," he murmured. "Still years too young. Do you know how old I am, Teddi?"

"You . . . you're thirty-three," she whispered.

"Thirty-four," he corrected. His eyes fell to her mouth and studied it for a long time. "God, what a sweet mouth!" he ground out. Then, as if the admission had annoyed him, he let her go abruptly and moved away toward the front door.

She stood staring helplessly after him, her eyes glued to the blue-patterned shirt stretched across his broad shoulders, the blond head that seemed to throw off golden lights as he passed under the chandelier. She loved the way he walked, so tall and bronzed and regal. She loved everything about him.

He turned with the doorknob in hand and looked back at her suddenly, reading with pinpoint accuracy the aching hunger she was too young to disguise.

His face hardened. His hand tightened on the doorknob. He uttered a soft curse and whirled, slamming the door shut with a booted foot as he headed straight for her.

She watched him with eyes so filled with confusion they seemed black, her face lifting as he came closer.

She didn't even protest when he reached for her, crushing her soft breasts against his chest as he bent to find her mouth in one smooth, expert motion.

She felt his hard lips burrow into hers with a sense of awe, her eyes closing so that she could savor their warmth and sensuality. She stiffened involuntarily as he tried to deepen the kiss, his tongue probing at her lips.

"Let me..." he ground out, grasping the hair at the nape of her neck to tug gently, surprising a gasp from her lips. As they parted, his tongue shot past them into the soft, dark warmth of her mouth, exploring, tasting, teasing, fencing with her own tongue in an intimacy she'd never liked with other men. But King made of it a pleasure beyond bearing, a caress so sensuous that her hands reached up to grasp his hard face between them and urge him even closer.

She moaned achingly at the penetration, the suggestive intimacy as his tongue thrust gently into her soft mouth.

He reached down, half lifting her body against his so that she could feel every warm, hard line of it in total contact with her own.

"King," she whispered shakily.

He drew back for breath, dragging air into his lungs. His eyes fairly blazed as they searched hers. "Witch," he ground out. "Little dark-eyed witch, stop casting spells on me, will you?"

Even as he spoke, he freed her, turned on his heel and strode out the door. He slammed it violently behind him, while Teddi touched her swollen mouth with nervous fingers and trembled deliciously with delayed reaction. Years of waiting, hoping, to feel that hard, arrogant mouth on her own, and it had finally happened. King had kissed her. The crazy thing was that the reality had been so much more wonderful than the dream....

Chapter Four

Teddi walked around in a daze for the rest of the day, absently listening to Jenna rave about Blakely while her mind lingered on the hard, possessive crush of King's mouth.

"Do you realize what you just agreed to do?" Jenna asked as they helped Mary put supper on the table.

"Ummmm?" Teddi offered with an empty smile.

Jenna grinned. "You agreed to have cowhide biscuits with grass sauce and ride a saddled chicken."

The flush appeared instantly in Teddi's cheeks and she averted her eyes to the platter of biscuits she was putting on the table. "Sorry about that," she murmured. "I guess my mind wasn't on what you were saying."

"It's been conspicuous by its absence all afternoon," came the dry reply. "Uh, that wouldn't have anything to do with King being home?"

The platter lurched precariously as it met the tabletop. "Why ever would you think that?" Teddi asked, innocent eyes dark and wide.

"Joey walked out of the office carrying his duffel bag an hour ago."

Teddi blinked.

Jenna hid a giggle behind a slender hand. "Every time King goes broody, he takes a strip off Joey. Then Joey packs his duffel bag and gives notice. The last time he did that," she continued, "was at Easter. I told you the men started getting nervous the minute you set foot on the place."

Teddi just stared, her heart beating a tattoo as she suddenly heard the front door open and close with a bang.

Mary's clear voice could be heard in the hall. "Oh, there you are, dear, the girls are putting the food on the table now."

"The computer broke down," came the harsh reply, accompanied by the sound of angry footsteps, "and we can't get a repairman here before morning. But I need those herd records *now!*"

"What are you going to do?" Mary was asking.

"Fix it," he growled. There were sounds of paper rustling, drawers opening and closing. "If I can find the repair manual ... there's a home number for one of the service technicians in it. They don't give you schematics or troubleshooting info, you have to call a service technician! Before long, you'll have to call a number in Ontario in order to engage the gears of your automobile...don't keep supper, I'll be late." And the door slammed loudly.

"It's Saturday night," Teddi murmured. "Surely to goodness he doesn't expect a service technician to fly out here on a Saturday night...?"

Jenna eyed her friend patiently. "Would you say no to him?" she asked.

There was a brief pause. "I think I'd pack my duffel bag," she admitted with a grin.

Mary came through the door just then, her eyes widening at the amount of food on the table. "Gracious, what army are you girls planning to feed tonight?" she gasped, her eyes going from the platter of biscuits Teddi had made to the ham casserole, cottage-fried potatoes, green beans, sliced carrot sticks and celery and tomatoes with a dip, and the enormous banana pudding on the elegant table under the crystal chandelier.

"It'll keep until tomorrow," Jenna promised, winking at Teddi.

Mary laughed. "What a pity King's going to miss this," she murmured as she sat down and unfolded her napkin. "All his favorites. Buttering him up, Jenna?" she mused.

"Actually, it was Teddi's idea to do the casserole," came the dry reply. "I can't make one, you know. And look at these biscuits!"

"Never mind, my friend," Teddi murmured as she spooned the casserole onto her plate. "I love it, too, as it happens."

It was late, and the women were watching an old movie on TV in the den when King came in. He looked every year of his age. His thick blond hair was rumpled, and his shirt was open at the throat. His face was hard, but there was a faint satisfaction in it as he went directly to the bar and poured himself a whiskey before he dropped into his armchair with a sheaf of papers in one hand.

"I see you got the repairman, dear," Mary remarked.

"An obliging gentleman," King agreed, fingering the glass as he scanned an open folder in his lap. "I'm going to cull a few cows, and I needed these records before I made a decision on which ones to sell."

"Tomorrow is Sunday," Mary reminded him.

"Ummm," he agreed. "But Jake Harmone is driving over here tomorrow morning before church to make me an offer. Hence the urgency."

"Sell Mahitabel and I'll never speak to you again," Jenna promised him.

He looked up with the old, mischievous light in his silvery eyes as he locked glances with his sister. "Mahitabel hasn't calved in six years," he reminded her. "She's eating my grass, drinking my spring water and yielding absolutely nothing."

"She's tough," Jenna replied.

"So she is," King murmured thoughtfully. "But if we parboiled her first . . ."

"King!" Jenna positively shrieked. "You can't, you wouldn't!"

He burst out laughing at her horrified expression. "All right, calm down. I'll put it off another year, as I've done for the past six."

His sister breathed easier. "What a scare you gave me!"

"I'll remind you again that sentimentality and cattle raising don't mix," he remarked.

"As I found out at the tender age of twelve," Jenna said, pouting, "when my pet bull disappeared."

"He was an Angus," King reminded her.

"So? What's wrong with black Angus?" she challenged.

"Nothing, except that we run Herefords," he replied. "Your pet got in with my registered cows and they dropped half Angus calves the next spring."

"I thought they were cute," Jenna said defensively. "Little black calves with white faces."

"If you had your way, you'd make pets of every calf on the place," King murmured indulgently. His eyes shifted suddenly and met Teddi's. Something flashed briefly in the gray depths and burned so brightly that she dropped her own gaze and tried unsuccessfully to calm her wildly beating heart. Involuntarily, her mind caught and held the image of King's hard mouth taking hers, and a shimmer of pure pleasure washed over her.

"Well, the hero got the girl. As usual." Mary got up with a sigh and turned off the television. "I hate to leave good company, but that shopping spree left me dragging. Good night, my dears," she said with a motherly smile, bending to kiss Jenna's cheek as she went out the door.

"Do you still type?" King asked Teddi unexpectedly.

"Uh . . . yes," she stammered.

He got up from the chair with the folder in one big hand. "Come help me make a list, then."

"Aren't you going to have something to eat?" Jenna asked him, glancing curiously from King's set face to Teddi's flushed one.

"Later, honey," he said, ruffling her hair as he went out the door.

Jenna winked at Teddi, her whole face beaming with mischief as her friend followed him.

Teddi perched herself at one side of the big oak desk in King's pine-paneled study and tapped out the cattle names and lineage and herd numbers and pasture locations while he leaned back in his big chair and dictated them, ending each notation with the cow's production record. She began to realize that the names he was giving her—or rather, the numbers that seemed to pass for names for most of them—were those of cows that didn't produce calves that were up to his exacting standards.

"Animal slavery," she mumbled as he finished, and she paused to make a correction.

He raised both heavy blond eyebrows and glanced at her. "I beg your pardon?"

"Selling off cows," she explained, a tiny mischievous light in her wide brown eyes. "Poor things, what if that Mr. Harmone beats them or doesn't feed them properly?"

"Mr. Harmone," he informed her, "is going to use them as hosts for embryo transplants. They're Herefords, but they'll throw purebred black Angus calves."

She stared at him. "Sure they will," she agreed. "Shouldn't you eat something? Lack of food . . ."

He grimaced, getting up to toss the records on his desk. "My God, don't you know anything about cattle breeding?"

She nodded. "First you take a boy cow . . ."

He chuckled deeply, watching the lights play in her short, thick hair, almost blue-black in its darkness. "It's not quite that simple, darling. Suffice it to say that this new technique has a large following and Mr. Harmone is part of it. You take purebred embryos and transplant them into host cattle—like these Herefords. The result is a well-cared-for purebred calf with superior bloodlines out of a less expensive cow."

"Improving on nature?" she asked with lifted eyebrows.

"Don't women do it all the time?" he fired back, looming over her. "Lipstick, eye shadow, curlers . . . none of which applies to you right now, however," he conceded, studying her impossibly clear, creamy

complexion, the wide, black-lashed eyes that stared up
at him.

"I don't use makeup when I'm not working," she
murmured. Her eyes were as busy as his, seeking out
the hard angles of his face, his imposing nose, his
deep-set gray eyes, his chiseled mouth and square chin.
He was so good to look at. Her first sight of him, all
those years ago, had made him like a narcotic to her.
She could scarcely exist without the picture of him in
her mind, her heart. Her eyes fed on him.

The mention of her modeling had been enough to
break the fragile peace between them. King's face had
gone hard; his eyes glittered like sun on a rifle barrel.

"I saw one of those televised fashion shows you
were in," he remarked curtly. "They ran it on the ca-
ble station."

Her eyes avoided his probing stare. "I can imagine
what you thought of it."

"Can you? I've seen bikinis that showed less. One
of the blouses you wore was quite transparent, and
you wore nothing under it!"

Her face flamed. He was right, a great many of
David Sethwick's creative designs for Velvet Moth
were practically sheer and very sensuous. Working
around designers and other models, she tended to
forget that bodies were more than just mannequins to
people outside the business. King had such a low
opinion of Teddi, and all without foundation. She
wondered how he'd react if he knew how innocent she

truly was, how afraid she was of anything physical. . . .

"High fashion very often is . . . risqué," she had to acknowledge, studying her well-kept nails where they rested on the typewriter keys. "And I work primarily for two designers of evening wear. It's supposed to be sexy-looking."

"You damned sure wouldn't go anywhere with me in some of those dresses," he growled.

The thought of it made chills go down her spine. It was heady to think of spending an evening with King, being escorted by him to some grand dance. She sighed unknowingly. It would never happen. Not as long as King felt the way he did about her profitable sideline. Which she ought to be pursuing even now, she reminded herself, if she was going to make enough to handle her school fees for the rest of the year. Velvet Moth would make sure she had work while she was in New York, and so would Lovewear—designers at both houses, fortunately, liked her style and her punctuality. And there was always the chance of one or two TV commercials.

"You love it, don't you?" he asked suddenly, perching himself on the edge of the desk to study her. He was far too close. She could feel the warmth of his big body, see the buttons straining at the open throat of his shirt as he shifted, smell the outdoorsy scent of him. Being this close made her feel trembly, just as it had this afternoon when he'd reached for her. . . .

"Love what?" she asked vaguely, looking up into his searching gray eyes.

He didn't answer for a minute, his gaze lingering on her wide, misty eyes, her full, parted lips, as if he found the sight of her at this range disconcerting. That was ridiculous, she told herself.

"Modeling," he said after a tense pause. "The glitter, the glamour, the night lights, the male adulation. You couldn't give it up if you tried, despite all that rot about becoming a teacher."

Her eyes flashed. "You don't really think I'm spending so much time in college just to improve my modeling technique?" she challenged.

"I'll admit you baffle me," he said quietly. "Why teaching?"

"Why not? It's an honorable profession," she said with deliberate nonchalance.

"Where would you teach?" he persisted. "College?"

"Grammar school," she corrected, her eyes lighting up at the mental picture she had of guiding young hands toward new pursuits. "Kindergarten, if possible."

His face underwent a remarkable change. He took a deep breath. "You like children?"

Her face beamed. "Oh, yes," she told him genuinely. "Especially when they're just old enough to reach out and begin to experience the world around them."

His chest rose and fell heavily as he stared down into her wide, dark eyes. His tanned hand moved, touching her cheek, and she trembled at the light touch. It was amazing, the sensations he caused when he touched her. She wasn't nervous of King like this, although she still had deep fears of any man in an intimate way. It was highly unlikely, of course, that King would ever want to be intimate with her, but she couldn't help being curious about her own responses. She liked the feel of his hard, warm mouth against hers, she even liked the intimacy of his tongue. But to feel his hard fingers against her bare skin...would she panic, as she had before when one of her dates tried to go further than kisses? Part of her was insatiably curious about King in that way.

"You fascinate me," he murmured absently. His thumb brushed across her full, soft lips, parting them while he held her eyes with his. "Half woman, half child...and so exquisitely beautiful."

"I'm...not beautiful," she protested weakly. Her heart beat violently as his face moved closer.

"Oh, but you are," he breathed. His mouth poised just over hers, his warm, whiskey-scented breath mingling with hers, his eyes riveted to the curve of her lips. "I was afraid this would happen. Once wasn't enough. Not nearly enough.

His fingers tilted her chin at just the angle he wanted, and she watched, fascinated, as his hard mouth parted just before it touched hers. She waited, aching, with time stretched to the tautness of a violin string between them.

The sudden opening of the door was no less cruel than the flick of a whip. King lifted his head with a harsh jerk, his eyes almost black with frustration as he watched his sister come in with a loaded tray.

Teddi bit hard on her lip to keep from crying out, so desperately had she wanted that kiss. But she had years of practice at hiding her real feelings, and she looked quite calm when Jenna got to the desk with sandwiches and coffee.

"I thought you might be hungry," Jenna explained with a grin at her taciturn brother. "Slave driver, isn't he?" she asked Teddi.

"My God, real slices of ham," King burst out, lifting the edge of one of the sandwiches.

"Mama does skimp, doesn't she?" Jenna laughed. "This was all the ham that was left. Teddi made a ham casserole for dinner tonight and that took the rest."

King's piercing eyes swung to Teddi, lingering on her flushed face. "Ham casserole?" he murmured.

She lifted her chin. "I like it," she said defensively.

One corner of his chiseled mouth curled sensuously. "Do you?"

He knew she'd made it especially for him, the beast, but she wasn't going to let him see any reaction from her. "If you're through, I think I'll turn in," she said as she rose, muffling a yawn she didn't feel.

He hesitated just an instant, reading quite accurately the apprehension in her wide, dark eyes.

"That's all I need, thanks. For tonight," he added, and she knew he wasn't talking about herd records.

"Coming up, Jenna?" Teddi asked her friend with practiced carelessness as she went toward the door.

"Right behind you. Say, Blakely and I are going into Calgary in the morning. Want to. . . ?"

"She's going to Banff with me," King broke in.

Startled, Teddi's bright eyes shot to his face and were captured by his hard, unblinking gaze.

"I've got to talk business with a man up there tomorrow afternoon. I thought Teddi might like to see the park. Since none of us have ever thought to take her there," he added carelessly, although the look in his eyes was anything but careless.

"I . . . I'd like that," Teddi heard herself saying. It was like being handed a special present without asking for it.

"You won't throw her off the mountain or anything?" Jenna teased with lifted brows.

King actually laughed. "No, I won't throw her off the mountain. Satisfied?"

"You can't be surprised that I asked," Jenna countered, escorting her friend to the door. "Only a few days ago, you hated the idea of having her here."

King studied Teddi's slight figure, letting his intent gaze move lazily up to her flushed face and thick, short hair. "That was a few days ago," he murmured.

"It's overwork," Teddi assured her puzzled friend. "Too many computer breakdowns and skipped meals." She leaned closer and said in a loud, conspiratorial whisper, "Just ask him about having Herefords produce purebred black Angus cattle."

Jenna stared, gaping, at her older brother.

He tossed his thick, blond hair back with an impatient hand. "Don't ask," he warned, "unless you want to spend the next thirty minutes having it explained to you."

Jenna chuckled, pushing Teddi out the door. "I think you'd better eat your sandwiches, brother mine, and see if it doesn't help." And she closed the door behind her before he had a chance to reply.

"King, taking you to Banff?" Jenna laughed when they were upstairs. "My gosh, miracles happen every day, don't they?"

"You aren't half as surprised as I was," Teddi said, pausing at the door to her room. "And I'm still not sure why. Maybe he wants some privacy so he can give me the devil and I won't have any hope of rescue."

"Maybe he's mellowing," Jenna suggested.

"Maybe the chickens will give milk."

"Well, he didn't sound sarcastic or anything."

Teddi smiled wistfully. "You didn't hear him before you came in. He was giving me a scolding about that televised fashion show I was in."

"How interesting," came the amused reply. "Because when we watched it, he sat there staring like a man possessed. He didn't take his eyes off you, and he didn't say a word."

"He was probably busy trying to think up nasty things to say about it the next time he saw me," she countered, flushing.

"That wasn't how he looked," Jenna murmured thoughtfully, recalling the strange, intense look in her brother's eyes at the time.

"How did he look?"

Jenna met Teddi's curious eyes levelly. "He looked like a starving man."

Teddi turned away before Jenna could see and question the wild color in her cheeks. "It was televised before dinner, wasn't it?" she murmured. "Well, good night. See you in the morning."

"Inevitably," came the gleeful reply. "Another fascinating chapter of your ongoing war with King. I wish you two got along better," she added, suddenly serious. "I can't understand why he's so down on you. He isn't like that about another single person."

"Maybe I remind him of a woman he used to hate."

Jenna shook her head. "There aren't that many women in his past. Very few in his present, too." She grinned. "And no one at all since Easter," she added. "I wonder why?"

"Good night!" Teddi said quickly, darting into her room.

She rose after a restless night, her eyes full of dreams and hopes. It was the most exciting morning she could remember, because the day promised a whole afternoon in King's company.

Time seemed to fly as they all went to church together, and Teddi stood next to King, listening to his deep, pleasant voice as they sang hymns in the same Presbyterian church where his father and mother had married years before.

And then, church was over, and Teddi was feeling as if she could conquer the world as she sat beside King in his low-slung black Ferrari on the way to Banff. Her eyes wandered restlessly from the winding road between sky-high pines to the jagged peaks of the Rocky Mountains against an azure sky.

"It's as big as the whole world," she murmured, spellbound. "Everything out here seems gigantic, and the air is so clean."

King chuckled softly. "Cleaner than most places, thanks to our provincial government. We have stringent basic environmental standards that new developers must meet, to preserve our clean water and skies."

"Georgia has a fine environmental protection division, too," Teddi replied, "and equally stringent air and water conservation requirements. We like to think they're some of the best in the nation."

He glanced at her. "I always associate you with New York," he murmured dryly, "despite that southern accent."

"Why, because I model?" she asked defensively. "It's just a job, King."

"A job is something one does out of necessity," he fired back without looking her way. "You model because you like the glamour of it and the excitement."

How wrong he was, she thought dejectedly. She modeled because it was the only profession she was suited to that would earn her enough to stay in school. Dilly gave her nothing toward her tuition. But, of course, King didn't know that, and probably wouldn't believe her if she told him so.

"Just don't forget," he continued coldly, "that the excitement won't last forever. Men don't necessarily marry their pretty playmates, you know."

"Now, just hold it a minute," she flared, turning in the bucket seat to glare at him. "I'm not any man's playmate, and I won't be."

"Holding out for marriage?" he asked contemptuously. "I suppose you might find a man somewhere who'd marry a girl like you."

Her eyes blazed in a face that was flushed with indignation. "It's very easy to make snap judgments about people," she reminded him. "You do prize circumstantial evidence, don't you? Although how you manage to construe modeling as prostitution is something I can't imagine!"

"It's a small world, darling," he replied, making a mockery of the endearment. "I have an acquaintance who knows a great deal about your night life."

"Night life!" she burst out. "My gosh, by the time I get back from a day of assignments in New York, the last thing I want or need is a long social calendar! All

I do at night is soak my tired feet and get ready for the next day's assignments. The only time I go out is on weekends.''

"Sure," he replied curtly.

"And just who is your mysterious informant?'' she asked pointedly.

"I'll introduce you one of these days soon," he replied mysteriously.

"I can't wait," she returned sarcastically. She turned away, folding her arms across her chest. The blouse she wore was a camisole top that criss-crossed over her small breasts and tied at the side. Its pale blue color contrasted with the white slacks she wore, and emphasized her dark eyes and hair, her exquisite complexion. But King hadn't even noticed how she was dressed. He'd been too busy digging up insults. And she'd had such hopes of mending the conflict between them today. When he'd asked her, *told* her, about the trip to Banff, she really thought he had more than insults in mind.

She stared out the window at the incredible height of the Rockies as they traveled down the valley and across the Canadian Pacific Railway to enter Banff.

Banff was a shopper's and diner's delight, chock-full of international shops, malls and restaurants. And all around were the impossibly high, jagged peaks of the Rocky Mountains, giant stone sentinels casting their majestic shadows on the green, lush valley where the Bow River wound like a crystal ribbon.

"It's awesome," Teddi whispered, her eyes peering up toward the craggy summits that practically surrounded the valley.

"Yes, it is," King agreed. "I've lived half of my life in the shadow of the Rockies, but they still take my breath away. I can imagine how the old French fur traders felt when they saw them for the first time."

She glanced at his profile, the set of his head, the arrogant tilt of it. "One of your ancestors was a fur trader," she recalled. "So was your mother's grandfather."

"I can see the question coming," he replied drily. "No, I don't look French, do I?"

She let her attention wander back to the sharp edges of the summits, where the timberline was clearly visible. "I didn't say anything," she protested.

"My maternal grandfather was French, Miss Curiosity," he told her, "but my paternal grandmother was Dutch. And I don't have to tell you which characteristics I inherited."

"Where are we going?" she asked, watching the small shops and restaurants whiz by as the Ferrari ate up the miles.

"I thought you might like to see the grand old lady of the mountains," he said obliquely as they crossed the bridge over the majestic Bow River.

"The who?" she asked.

"The Banff Springs Hotel," he replied. "The original hotel was built in 1888, and much of the credit for it goes to William Van Horne of the Canadian Pacific

Railway, who thought that a luxury hotel would increase tourism. The CPR expanded it up until 1910, when they began to rebuild it. Unfortunately a fire destroyed part of the old building, but it was scheduled for demolition anyway, and the new hotel was completed in 1928. I think you'll find the architecture unique," he added as the gigantic hotel began to loom up in the distance. He glanced at her intrigued expression. "Three architects produced what you see, and believe me, the interior is just as impressive. No expense was spared on materials or workmanship."

"Oh, it's beautiful!" she burst out enthusiastically, fascinated by the towering structure, which reminded her of a castle.

"You should see it at night," he replied, "with all the windows blazing with light. It's quite lovely." He pulled up in the parking lot and cut the engine. "I can't imagine why none of us ever thought to bring you here before."

"There was never time," she said, reaching for the door handle.

"Or we never made time," he replied, something harsh in his deep voice.

She let him guide her into the lobby of the majestic hotel, fascinated by the fossilized stone throughout and the bronze doors to the Alhambra Dining Room, where they had coffee and pie. She felt as if her feet were barely touching the ground when they walked back to the car. King had been polite, even courteous, and not a cross word had managed to get between them.

"Where to now?" she asked as she fastened her seat belt.

"You tell me," he corrected. "Would you like to go through some of the shops in town?"

"It's Sunday," she reminded him.

"And you'll find a number of them open, just the same," he promised. "Well?"

"I'd like that," she confessed.

"Typical woman," he mused, starting the car.

"I suppose you'd rather be hunting those poor moose and elk?" she teased.

"In season, yes, ma'am," he laughed. He glanced at her. "I like to ski, too. Do you?"

"I've never learned." Her eyes flickered away from his. "Well, Jenna hasn't, either!"

"If you spent much time around me, you'd learn plenty about skiing. And other things," he added, glancing sideways with a look that said more than words.

She avoided his eyes. "According to you, there isn't anything left for me to learn."

"And maybe I need to find out how much," he said softly.

She swallowed down the urge to leap out of the car and make a run for it. "Isn't the valley beautiful?" she asked politely.

He chuckled. "Yes, it is. When we've looked through Banff, we'll drive up to Lake Louise."

He pulled the car back out into the road, turning off presently to show her the magnificent gondola lift.

"We won't stop," he said, "but it's open year-round. There's even a restaurant and gift shop up there."

Up there was a long way off, and Teddi had no head for heights. "I don't think I'd ever make a skier if you have to start up there," she murmured.

"You'll never know until you try," he chuckled. "But we'll save that for another time. And there's always cross-country skiing," he added as he pulled back out into the main road. "We'll have to do that one winter."

The statement nagged in the back of her mind while King escorted her through one shop after another, showing her Indian handicrafts, Eskimo carvings and art work by native Western Canadian artists. The fur shop fascinated her, and so did the trading shop. King bought her a small carved totem that she knew she'd treasure as long as she lived, and two hours had gone by before she realized it.

They drove up to Lake Louise, traveling parallel to the Bow River on the long highway. Teddi gazed wide-eyed at the mountain scenery, drinking in fleeting glimpses of moose, mountain sheep, and craggy peaks that seemed to touch the clouds. Driving around Lake Louise was fascinating, too, she found.

"There, see the gondolas?" King nodded toward the lift.

"I'd rather look at the lake, if you don't mind," Teddi laughed, staring raptly out the window at it. "I'll bet you can hear the fish eating worms if you listen closely."

He pulled off the road and cut the engine. "Let's see," he told her, throwing his long legs out of the streamlined car.

She followed him down to the banks of the sky-blue lake and stood listening to the faint sloshing of the water at the shoreline, to the sound of the tall trees brushing each other in the breeze, to the far away baying of a hound.

She closed her eyes and she could almost see men in buckskins carrying flintlock rifles, on their way to check their trap lines. The air smelled of trees and water and bark and growing things, and her heart swelled.

"Daydreaming?"

She smiled as she opened misty eyes. "Sort of," she confessed.

"Picturing it as a site for a fashion show?" he chided.

She drew in a deep, slow breath, bending down to pick a blade of grass and worry it with her long fingers. "Actually, I was thinking about the men who settled this country," she said, "and the hardships they had to endure. There's so much history here."

"I know. I wasn't aware that you knew, however."

Her dark eyes were accusatory as they met his. "I do occasionally think of things other than expensive clothes and cameras. That part of my life exists only in New York. On campus, I'm a student and a restaurant employee. Here, I'm just me."

"Are you?" He wasn't wearing his ranch hat, and his thick, blond hair was caught by the wind, falling carelessly onto his broad forehead as he stared down at her.

She met his piercing gray eyes squarely and felt the breath pour out of her at the impact.

The old tension was back between them, as suddenly, as unexpectedly, as it had been the night before when Jenna opened the door of King's den. Her heart fluttered like a wild bird as she stood there, feeling the nearness of his big body with every nerve in her own.

His eyes dropped to her neckline where the pale blue blouse crossed over her breasts. Because of the thin camisole straps, she hadn't bothered with a bra, and she could see King's eyes, intent and curious on the thin fabric.

"This bloody thing has haunted me all afternoon," he ground out, moving a step closer, his voice deep and slow. "Are you wearing anything at all under it?"

"King!" she burst out, breathless.

"Just like a woman," he grumbled, reaching out to catch her shoulders and draw her closer, "to wear something that drives a man around the bend and then be shocked when he notices it."

"I didn't . . . didn't wear it to drive you around any bends," she protested.

"Didn't you, Teddi bear?" he murmured. One big hand pressed against her back, urging her close, while the other slid deftly, expertly, under one strap of the camisole blouse, making exquisite sensations where it touched the silken flesh of her shoulder, her collarbone.

"Your skin feels like velvet," he whispered. His fingers spread out, warm and hard and faintly calloused, lifting so that the blouse and her bare flesh parted company and the breeze touched her like a lover's hand.

She gasped, trembling, as his fingers edged nearer to one small, taut breast.

"Look at me," he breathed gruffly, his voice so commanding that she instantly obeyed it. "I want to watch you."

"King . . ." she whispered his name, not knowing if it was a protest or a plea.

"I've wanted to touch you like this until I ache with it," he whispered, letting his eyes drop to the silky blouse, deliberately lifting the edge to reveal the pale, hard-tipped breasts to his fiery eyes.

She heard his intake of breath and knew in that instant that she was lost, that he could take anything he wanted and there was no way on earth she could stop him. . . .

Her shocked eyes met his, her lips parted under a rush of breath. His hand began to move and he watched the wildness burn in her eyes as their gazes locked. She was spellbound, her heart throbbing as she tensed, waiting helplessly for the agonizingly slow descent of his hard, teasing fingers. . . .

Chapter Five

"Oh, gee, Mom, what a great spot for a picnic!" came the sudden, devastating cry from the car neither Teddi nor King had heard pull off the road and stop.

King jerked as if he'd been hit in the back, both hands lifting to pull Teddi's forehead to his damp chest, his broad back protecting her from prying eyes as she fought down tears of absolute frustration.

She was trembling, and his hands soothed her, although they seemed none too steady. His breathing was as erratic as hers.

"It's all right, darling," he whispered over her head. "It's all right. Hold on to me."

She clung to his shirt, hating her own weakness and his knowledge of it.

His hand smoothed the hair from her hot cheek. "I wanted it just as much as you did, little one," he whispered. "Don't be embarrassed."

"Afternoon!" a friendly voice called from nearby. "Marvelous view, isn't it?"

"Marvelous," King replied politely. "Having a picnic?"

"Sure are! Uh, on your honeymoon?" the voice mused.

King chuckled. "Not quite," he murmured, leaving the other man to draw his own conclusions.

"Lovely day for sightseeing, isn't it?" a female voice broke in, followed by several younger voices that seemed to split the air and then faded gradually away.

"You can come up for air now," King murmured. "They're out of sight."

She swallowed nervously and lifted her head, avoiding his amused eyes as she moved away from him. "Could we get a cup of coffee somewhere, do you suppose?" she asked in an abnormally high-pitched tone.

"I could use a whiskey myself," he murmured, "but I suppose coffee will do. How about some fondue? There's a restaurant in Banff that specializes in it."

"I'd enjoy that," she said, following him back to the car. "But what about that man you were supposed to see on business?" she asked, remembering his appointment.

He looked puzzled for an instant. "Man? Business? Oh, him," he muttered. "Well, I'll see him another day. It's too bloody late now."

Which made her feel even worse, as if she'd carried him out of his way and wasted his time. He was taut as a drawn cord all the way into Banff and the sound of the radio was like a wall between them. Just for an instant she wondered if frustration could be causing his strange silence. But, then, he'd only been teasing, hadn't he? As usual.

He didn't say a word until they were seated in the fondue house drinking coffee and enjoying a special Swiss cheese fondue while music played softly around them.

She dunked her bread into the fondue, almost losing it, and noticed King watching her with a peculiar smile.

"You'd better be careful," he cautioned. "Or don't you know the tradition about fondue?"

She shook her head, her eyes dark and wide in the soft light.

"If a woman drops something in the pot," he said softly, watching her, "she has to surrender a kiss to the men at the table."

Her cheeks began to color delicately. "And if a man does the same?"

"He's obliged to buy a round," he replied. His eyes studied her face, her soft, red mouth. "We seem fated to be interrupted at all the wrong times."

Shaken, she tried to dunk another bread cube, but her hand trembled so much as she lifted the fork that she dropped the cube squarely into the pot, which embarrassed her even more.

"If I were conceited," he murmured, fishing it out for her with his own fork, and offering it to her, "I might think you did that on purpose."

She took the cube between her lips, and saw him watching the movement with an intensity that was shattering. She averted her eyes.

"I'm afraid I don't have any illusions about the way you think of me," she said, subdued, as she sipped her hot coffee.

He finished his own bread cubes and sat back. His thick blond hair caught the light and turned silvery in it, matching the glitter of his eyes. "How do I think of you, honey?" he asked.

"As a flighty, money-mad tramp," she replied.

He fingered his coffee cup thoughtfully. "You haven't done much to satisfy my curiosity about you."

"Why bother?" she asked. "You wouldn't believe anything I said, you never have. You hated me on sight five years ago."

One corner of his disciplined mouth lifted wryly. "Not quite."

"At any rate," she continued, "you didn't want me on the place, and I knew it. I seem to have spent most of my vacations and holidays since I met Jenna dodging either her invitations or you."

"Was that the only reason—because you thought I had it in for you?"

She looked into her coffee cup. "Of course."

"You little liar," he accused softly.

She took a large swallow of coffee. "Shouldn't we get back to the ranch now?" she asked quickly.

He caught her eyes and searched them intently. The silence between them was broken only by the soft murmur of other diners' conversations.

"I thought you were going to pass out when I started to touch you earlier," he said in a deep, hushed tone. "Why are you afraid of me?"

"I'm not," she replied firmly, avoiding his eyes. "You . . . you caught me by surprise, that's all."

"I rather think I did," he murmured. He didn't pursue it, but his eyes were calculating.

All the way down the road, she felt his gaze on her while a tape played soft, soothing music that helped to calm her shattered nerves. She didn't even attempt conversation. She was too shaken by her own physical reactions to him to try.

They were just a few miles down the road from Gray Stag when a thunderstorm split the skies open, and King was forced to pull over onto the shoulder because the rain obscured the road completely.

Fortunately for Teddi, there wasn't much lightning. And the sound of the rain on the roof and hood of the sports car was soothing, oddly comforting. It made the interior of the car cozy and warm and isolated.

King leaned one arm over the back of her seat, staring openly at her, letting his eyes trace every soft line of her body in a silence that was intensified by the fury of the rain.

"Not frightened?" he asked softly, lighting a cigarette with steady fingers.

"There's no lightning," she murmured evasively.

"I remember a night when there was a lot of it," he said thoughtfully, opening a window slightly to let the smoke escape. "You were sixteen or seventeen, and I heard you crying because of the storm."

She searched his narrowed, intent eyes. "When you opened the door, it was a toss-up as to whether I was more afraid of the lightning or you."

He smiled faintly. "I realized that. It was a good thing for you that I did," he added, the smile fading. His eyes dropped to the filmy bodice of her blouse, narrowing. "There was precious little to the gown you were wearing that night. When the light hit you at a certain angle, it was transparent." His eyes lifted to catch her shocked ones. "You didn't realize that, did you? The hardest thing I've done in years was open that door and walk out. I felt as if a wall had fallen on me."

She averted her gaze to the rain splattering on the spotless hood, silently counting the drops. Her face had gone red and she couldn't look at him. She hadn't known the gown was transparent, she'd been too afraid of the storm.

"You haven't changed," he said absently, watching her. "Your body is as perfect now as it was then. Pink and creamy—"

She caught her breath, remembering his eyes on her. "Don't," she pleaded.

"Will you stop this prudish act?" he growled suddenly, flinging the cigarette out the window before he turned to catch her shoulders and drag her across the console into his hard, warm arms.

At his sudden proximity, her senses exploded, and all she could do was lie stiffly against his warm chest and stare helplessly into his blazing eyes.

"One thing's for certain," he breathed roughly as his arms tightened. "No one's going to interrupt us right now. I ache like a boy for you!"

His mouth came down on hers roughly, forcing her lips apart. She gasped, frightened at his passion. Her arms strained against him, but he was far too strong to be moved, and far too hungry. She couldn't tear her mouth away, she couldn't free herself.

Suddenly, it was like that other night, the night when she was fourteen, and one of her aunt's lovers had tried to seduce her. She could still feel the thick, wet lips on hers, the roughness of his hands touching her where none of her boyfriends had dared to touch, hurting her. She'd been helpless then, too, terrified and disgusted and sick. And if her aunt hadn't suddenly come home, if he hadn't heard her key in the lock, it might have been worse than it was. But he had heard, and had let Teddi go, daring her to tell her aunt.

She'd groped her way to her room, her clothes torn, her body bruised and hurt, and cried herself to sleep. Hating him. Hating all men, for the animals they became when they were woman-hungry.

And now it was that night all over again, and he was hurting her, trying to force her....

The wild little scream and the violent crying got through to King. He released her, drawing back quickly to look down into her pale, frightened face.

"Teddi?" he murmured huskily.

She was trembling from head to toe, huge tears rolling silently down her cheeks, her mouth trembling from the sobs that shook the rest of her.

King's dark face contorted. One big hand brushed gently at the tears, then at her tousled hair, soothing, comforting.

"It's all right," he said softly, in a voice far too tender to be King's. "It's all right, honey, it's all right. I'm not going to hurt you. I should have known, but you wouldn't tell me...here, now, stop crying."

She was as stiff as a rod while he wiped the tears away, and there was a new wariness in her big brown eyes as they met his. "I'm...I'm not that kind...of woman," she whispered brokenly. "You...treated me like a tramp...."

He caught his breath, his face hardening even as she watched. "I know."

She pushed at his chest. "Please...let me go."

He hesitated for a moment, his eyes wavering. But then he loosened his tight grip and she moved back

against the door, like a small animal at bay, feeling all
over again the insolence of his mouth, his tongue, the
rough contempt of his hands on her body, burning
even through the fabric.

He pulled a cigarette from his pocket and lit it.

She licked her suddenly dry lips. "May...may I have
one, please?" she asked.

He looked surprised. "You don't smoke."

"You don't carry a bottle of liquor around with
you," she said simply, trying to smile, but not suc-
ceeding.

Frowning, he pulled out a second cigarette and lit it
for her. She took it without making contact with his
hard fingers and dragged on it, almost choking herself before she got the hang of it.

He watched her intently, his eyes running from her
untidy hair, over her pale cheeks to her mouth and
lower, to her rumpled blouse.

"Why didn't you tell me in the beginning that you
were a virgin?" he asked quietly, studying her.

"Because I had no idea you were going to make a
pass at me," she said weakly. "And you wouldn't have
believed me if I'd told you."

He sighed. "After the way you looked on the lake-
shore, I just might have." He studied her flushed
cheeks. "Did I hurt you?"

The flush got worse. She shook her head jerkily.
"Please, can we go back to Gray Stag now?"

"Teddi..." He moved closer, and she backed against the door, her eyes impossibly wide, her body rigid in helpless reaction.

He stopped short and something like a shadow passed over his face before he turned back to the steering wheel and started the car. He glanced at her as he pulled back into the road, saw her slight figure relax visibly, and frowned thoughtfully. Then they were underway again, with only the radio to break the silence that lasted until they reached Gray Stag.

"Did he start on you again?" Jenna asked as they went upstairs that night.

Teddi only nodded, going into her room, aware that Jenna had followed.

Jenna closed the door and sat down on Teddi's blue coverlet, her hands folded, watching her friend pause by the darkened window and stare blankly out of it.

"And what else?" Jenna pursued. "You come back home looking like a ghost, King goes out and doesn't come back...even mother, bless her, noticed something was wrong."

"I can't talk about it," Teddi whispered. She sighed. "Jenna, I think I'd better go back to New York in the morning."

"No!" Jenna jumped to her feet and caught Teddi's hands. There was sadness in her whole look. "You've got to tell me what happened. Did he make a pass at you?"

Teddi tried not to answer, but her own hesitation, the fright in her eyes gave her away.

"You never told him what happened to you, did you?" Jenna asked knowingly, nodding when she read the answer in Teddi's wide, haunted brown eyes.

"Tell King? Give him a stick to hit me over the head with?" Teddi moaned. "He would have accused me of tempting the man, and you know it! He thinks I'm a tramp, and that's how he treated me today."

"Oh, Teddi," Jenna said sympathetically. "I think you underestimate King all the way around. Frankly I can't see him making a pass at a woman he hates, it isn't in character. He's not a playboy, and he's much too intense for love games."

Teddi turned away. "No, he's not," she mumbled darkly. "He hates me, all right, he's shown me that. And now I've got to go away, don't you see?"

"At least wait until morning before you make any decisions," Jenna pleaded, her face worried. "I know you're upset, but sleep on it, please?"

"It won't change anything," Teddi told her.

"You don't know that." She caught Teddi by the arms and shook her gently, smiling. "Maybe King will decide to spend the rest of his life in Australia, have you considered that? Maybe he's packing right now."

Teddi couldn't help smiling, too. "I'm sure he is," she muttered. "I can just see your brother running from a woman."

"Hasn't he been running from you for years?" Jenna asked softly. "Sleep well. Things will work themselves out, truly they will. Good night."

Teddi paced the room after Jenna had left. Sleeping on it wouldn't help; she couldn't stay if King was going to treat her so shabbily. She'd wondered how she'd react to him if he ever made a pass, and now she knew. She'd panicked. But...but she hadn't down by the lake, when he'd touched her so gently, caressed her so tenderly. She hadn't been afraid, she'd wanted more. She folded her arms across her chest and sighed. If only he hadn't come on so strong, perhaps she could have given him the response he wanted. She would have held nothing from him if he'd just been gentle.

Now she was faced with going back to that empty apartment sooner than she planned. What if Dilly was there? Dilly was nobody's idea of a mother. Saddled with the responsibility of caring for her brother's child, Dilly had never liked Teddi. And when she'd broken with her boyfriend, he'd told her all sorts of lies about Teddi leading him on. That had placed a wall between them that had never come down. It never would, if Teddi knew her aunt. She'd be so glad when her education was completed and she could strike out on her own.

She put on her nightgown and got into bed. She wouldn't think about it, not about Dilly or King or the future, she told herself. But she did. And the night was the longest she'd spent in many long years.

She was up long before the rest of them the next morning, finding the kitchen deserted when she went into it to make coffee.

Normally Miss Peake would have been busy making breakfast, but everyone had managed with toast and coffee in her absence. Up until now, Teddi thought, deciding that making breakfast might, in some magical way, help her make up her mind what to do.

She dug out bacon, eggs, and butter and two frying pans and got busy. While the bacon was frying, she made the huge cat's head biscuits that King liked, and had them ready to go in the oven when the bacon was done. While the biscuits cooked, she made a huge platter of scrambled eggs, and by then the coffee was ready as well.

She was setting the table when King walked in and stopped short in the doorway.

He was devastatingly masculine in his jeans and denim shirt. She glanced at him quickly and turned her attention back to the table, her heart beating madly.

"If you wouldn't mind calling the others," she said quietly, "I'm just putting breakfast on the table."

"You're not a servant in this house," he said curtly.

She glared back at him, and suddenly her mind was made up. "I know that, but I'd like a good breakfast before I catch my flight and as I'm sure you've noticed, Miss Peake isn't here to cook it."

"What flight?" He stood stock-still, watching her.

"My flight to New York." She turned to go back into the kitchen.

He followed, his boots making harsh thuds as he walked. "Cancel it," he said.

She glanced at him from the coffeepot, where she was filling cups. "I will not." How could she, anyway, when she hadn't made a reservation yet?

"Then I will."

She set the pot down, hard. "I won't be held prisoner!"

"I want you to stay," he said quietly.

The faint emphasis on "I" froze her. She looked into eyes that stared back with unnerving intensity, faintly bloodshot, as if he hadn't slept any better than she had.

"Why?" she asked softly. "So you can start on me all over again? Carry on where you left off yesterday?"

He drew in a slow breath, ramming his hands into his jean pockets as he leaned back against the wall and stared at her. "I found out everything I wanted to know about you yesterday," he said. "Every single thing, in the one way I could without the risk of being lied to. I didn't mean to frighten you quite so badly, but I wanted answers you wouldn't have given me any other way."

She stiffened. "You mean you did that on purpose?"

He nodded solemnly. "It was a revelation. I had a feeling that you weren't half as sophisticated as I'd given you credit for being. The first time I kissed you, I had to force you to open your mouth—hardly the response of a woman who knows much about kissing,'' he added with a faint smile. ''And you were far too devastated by what happened at the lake, as if it was something totally new. It all added up to one thing. When I kissed you on the way home, the way you reacted clinched it. What I didn't bargain for,'' he added on a weary sigh, ''was the fear. Surely to God you knew I wouldn't force you?''

''No,'' she admitted, turning back to the coffee-pot. ''I didn't know that. You...you were so rough.''

''Someday you might understand why,'' he told her. ''But I don't think I'll try to explain it right now.''

He was across the room in three long strides, his nearness sudden enough to be startling. She could feel the heat from his body, feel his warm, smoky breath stirring the hair at her temples, but still he didn't touch her.

She looked up apprehensively, helpless in the pull of his silvery eyes.

''I don't want you to go,'' he said quietly. ''Now that I know the truth, I'll never handle you so roughly again.''

Kindness from him was so new that it was startling. ''But we're enemies,'' she whispered.

A muscle flinched in his square jaw. ''We were,'' he agreed.

''You don't even like me,'' she persisted. ''Why keep me around to irritate you even more?''

His face relaxed a little. One big, long-fingered hand came out of his pocket to touch, gently, the soft line of her cheek. "Because, little one," he murmured, "I like the way it makes me feel when I touch you."

Her cheeks flamed. Her lips parted. "Don't..."

He bent, brushing his lips over her forehead, her eyelids, her eyebrows in a silent caress that tingled with sensation. The whispery touch made her knees feel rubbery.

"You see?" he asked softly, drawing back to catch her stunned expression. "I'm not always rough."

She gazed up at him, fascinated, her eyes wide and very dark and curious.

His breath came roughly as he met that look, and like a man in a trance, his big hands came up to cup her face and hold it up to his.

"Come close," he breathed, bending toward her again. "I won't hurt you."

She obeyed him because the temptation was too much to resist. She loved the feel of his big body against hers, its strength and warmth; she loved the touch of his calloused hands against the tender skin of her face. She loved so much about him....

He brushed his mouth tenderly over hers, smoothing it, teasing it, and she caught her breath at the exquisite sensation and drew back an inch.

"Don't draw away," he murmured, his thumbs caressing the corners of her mouth. "It won't be like yesterday. Come here, darling."

And this time, he made it sound like an endearment. His mouth pressed softly, gently against hers, not forcing it open, not exerting any kind of pressure at all. It was the gentlest kind of kiss, and everything womanly in her responded wildly to it.

She eased up on her tiptoes, her fingers resting against his warm chest, feeling the rise and fall of his heavy breathing. Her eyes closed as she increased the pressure of her own mouth, wanting something more, something . . . more!

"Please . . . please," she begged, uncertain herself what she was asking of him.

"Are you sure?" he whispered against her pleading mouth. "It won't be this tender if I kiss you the way you're asking to be kissed."

Her eyes lazily slid open and looked up into his. "Oh, yes," she breathed shakily, "I'm sure . . ."

His fingers tightened at the sides of her head, his own eyes slitted and fairly blazed with hunger. "Open your mouth for me, darling," he whispered, and she felt his own lips parting even as he spoke, felt the moist insistence of them on her yielding mouth. Her eyes closed. The world began to spin around deliciously as she felt his tongue caressing the inner sweetness of her lips. . . .

This slow, sweet ardor was a world away from the rough passion of yesterday, even though he was hungry, and the hard crush of his mouth showed how hungry. But there was enough restraint in him to make her feel protected, secure in the warmth of his arms as he rocked her gently against his big body.

The sound of a door slamming brought his head up with a gruff curse. He drew in a steadying breath and reluctantly let her go. "I'm beginning to think there's no privacy in the world anymore," he muttered darkly.

Remembering their bad luck yesterday and the day before, she couldn't hold back a smile.

He shook her gently by the waist. "Think it's funny?" His eyes gleamed wickedly. "Come riding with me. If you dare."

"I don't know," she murmured thoughtfully, surprised at their suddenly easy relationship. "Isn't it supposed to be terribly dangerous going off into the woods with men?" She peeked up at him through impossibly long, thick lashes.

He caught his breath at the look, his fingers tightening. "Only for women who look like you do," he returned curtly. "Teddi..."

"Teddi, are you in there?" Jenna called suddenly.

King let go just as the door opened and Jenna walked in, her face beaming, her long hair swinging gaily. She stopped short at the sight of her taciturn brother and her flushed friend.

"Scrambled eggs at twenty paces?" Jenna guessed, looking from one to the other. "Or is it a duel with crossed forks?"

King smiled faintly. "Not quite. Here, I'll carry this in." He took up the platter of eggs and went into the dining room with it, leaving the girls to bring the coffee.

"Well?" Jenna prodded in an impatient whisper.

"We're going riding," Teddi said, shaking her head. "I don't ever expect to understand your brother."

"Oh, I think you might, someday," Jenna replied knowingly as they went through into the dining room, where Mary and King were already seated.

All through breakfast, Teddi felt his gaze. Once, she looked up from her cup of coffee and stared straight into his steady gray eyes. She didn't move and neither did he, and the air between them sizzled with emotion. He was, she thought wildly, such an impossibly attractive man. She wanted the wildest things—to sit down in his lap, and twine her fingers through that thick, blond hair, to trace his chiseled mouth and feather kisses all over his face. Her heart thudded furiously as she read the exact same hunger in his eyes, silver eyes that seemed to see right into her mind.

"Teddi, that was just delicious," Mary said, bringing her back to reality as she laid her fork down with a smile. "I didn't realize until this minute just how much I miss Miss Peake. Thank you."

"You're very welcome," Teddi replied, trying not to let the exploding emotions she was feeling show in her voice.

"At least the biscuits don't bounce," King observed, leaning back and cocking an amused eyebrow at her.

"King, what a thing to say!" Mary chided. "Why, I thought Teddi's first efforts were...admirable," she said, searching for a polite way to describe Teddi's attempts to make the same biscuits several years earlier.

"I've no quarrel with that," King replied. "They were admirable, all right." He stood up, flexing his broad shoulders absently. "But the biscuits still bounced."

Teddi couldn't repress a smile. "It wouldn't have been so bad if that Oklahoma cattleman hadn't been at the table," she murmured.

"And especially," Jenna couldn't resist adding, "after King had just been bragging about the delicious food Miss Peake was known for, unaware that Teddi had just had her first lesson in biscuit making."

"They *looked* lovely," Mary interrupted loyally.

"And now they're good enough to enter in bake-offs." Jenna smiled.

"Well, I get lots of practice," Teddi reminded her. "Since there aren't any modeling jobs to be had near the college, I work a split-shift at a restaurant," she told Mary. "My classes don't begin until late morning, so I'm up baking biscuits at 5 a.m. Then I go back and work another four hours after classes."

"What the devil for?" King demanded. "Your aunt supports you and pays your tuition. Do you need to kill yourself for spending money?"

"What do you mean, Dilly pays—" Jenna began hotly, until Teddi almost knocked over a chair trying to silence her.

"Never mind, Jenna," she said firmly, silently daring her friend to say another word. If King wanted to believe she was a girl who had to have money for frivolities, and a freeloader to boot, let him, she didn't care. "Excuse me," she said without meeting his eyes, and, putting down her napkin, left the room.

King caught up with her at the staircase, reaching out with a firm but gentle hand to catch her as she started up the steps toward her room.

"I didn't mean that the way you took it," he said before she could speak. His face looked harder than ever, his big body taut and poised, one booted foot on the step she was standing on.

She met his eyes, her look wary and uncertain. "I still have to have clothes to wear to classes," she said quietly. "And on some modeling assignments, I have to have my own wardrobe."

He drew in a deep breath. "And your aunt's generosity doesn't extend that far?"

He wouldn't have believed the extent of her aunt's "generosity," she thought bitterly, remembering that she had to buy her own clothes, pay her own tuition, and manage transportation to and from college. She was practically penniless after all that. But an education would give her the means to support herself, and she only had another year to go. Just one more year. Then she'd be totally independent of Dilly.

The hand on her arm was suddenly caressing, drawing her back down beside him. "We have a truce, remember?" he asked in a deep, lazy tone. "It shocked me to think of your doing something less glamorous than modeling. It always has. You don't look like a cook, darling."

"The biscuits prove I am one, though," she reminded him with a faint smile. "They don't bounce anymore."

He watched the light come back into her wide, dark eyes, and nodded. "So they don't. Come on. We'll ride up to the gate and back over by the Johnson property."

"Where all those gorgeous blue spruces are?" she asked.

"You always loved blue spruce, didn't you?" he laughed.

She nodded.

He smiled. "Still an outdoor girl, aren't you? Do you miss the city?"

She looked up at his rugged face under its shock of blond-streaked hair and saw blatant curiosity in his eyes. "No," she said truthfully. "I don't miss it at all."

He stared down at her so intensely that she felt as though her heart would run away with her. But a minute later, he tore his eyes away from hers and led her out the door.

Chapter Six

Riding around Gray Stag was one of Teddi's favorite recreations anytime, but riding with King beside her was a taste of heaven.

He looked magnificent in the saddle, she thought dreamily, glancing at the tall, broad-shouldered man beside her. In his well-fitting jeans and shirt, with a wide-brimmed hat cocked over one eye, shading his hard face, he was handsome enough to make any movie cowboy envious.

He took a draw from his cigarette and turned his head, catching her staring at him. One corner of his mouth curled and he chuckled softly at her embarrassment.

"The, uh, the scenery is lovely through here," she said, clearing her throat nervously.

"So are you, little one," he murmured appreciatively. "I don't mind if you look at me, Teddi. There's nothing to be embarrassed about."

He knew too much about women, she thought half angrily, trying to hold back a grin. She lost, and laughter burst out of her like the sun out of a thundercloud.

He reined in his horse and just looked at her, as if the gleeful, silvery laughter fascinated him. With the sun glinting off her dark hair, and the laughter making lights in her wide brown eyes, she was a sight to stop traffic.

"You make me feel about thirteen," she accused when she stopped to catch her breath. "And I do wish you'd stop making fun of me, it's not fair."

"I'm not making fun of you," he denied, smiling faintly. "I just like watching you blush, darling."

"Beast," she said, pouting.

He chuckled, urging his mount into a trot alongside her. "Have you seen my new Arabians?" he asked.

"No, we started that way, but Jenna and Blakely got side-tracked..."

His face hardened. "They're doing a lot of that lately," he muttered. "Blakely's slacking up on the job."

"King, he's a nice man," she began hesitantly, wary of disrupting the uneasy truce between them.

His cold gray eyes cut into hers. "You know how Jenna likes to spend money," he said curtly. "How long do you think the boy could support her tastes on his salary? Even if I gave him a tract in the Valley and helped him get started, it would be a hell of a job getting a foothold. He'd need a wife who could work alongside him, support him. Can you see my sister buckling down to that kind of drudgery, at her age?''

"I think Jenna is a lot like you," she said after a minute, choosing her words carefully. "I think she could do anything she wanted to do. And she loves Blakely.''

"She's infatuated with him," he corrected. "Girls your age don't know what love is.''

She averted her eyes. "Don't we?" she asked with faint bitterness, remembering all the sleepless nights she'd had because of the heartless man riding beside her.

"The fact is, Teddi bear," he concluded, "Jenna is my sister, and it's a family problem.''

She felt as if he'd hit her. Always an outsider, was that to be her destiny? "Thanks for reminding me that I'm not allowed a voice in your family matters," she said with cold dignity, refusing to look at him. "If you don't mind, I think I'll go on alone. I don't like the company I'm keeping." She wheeled her horse and rode back down the wide trail under the mammoth pines and spruces, along the wide bend in the river.

King caught up with her there and reached out to catch the reins and jerk her mount to a halt. "Get down," he said.

She didn't move. He dismounted gracefully, his eyes blazing, and jerked her down from the saddle into his hard arms.

"I want to go home," she burst out, seconds away from tears.

"Home is where I am," he said in a goading undertone. "Or haven't you worked that out yet?"

Before she could come up with any sane reply, he bent his head and took her mouth.

She barely felt him lift her into his arms. Her eyes were closed; her whole being was centered around the feel of his warm, hard mouth stroking between her full lips, preparing it, opening it to the piercing intimacy of his tongue.

She drank in the scent of him, the woodsy, smoky mingling of soap and cologne and tobacco, the hardness of his big body where her soft breasts were crushed into it as he carried her.

She felt herself being lowered, but she didn't open her eyes. She was too lost in the slow, tender ardor of his mouth to care where they were. She felt the pine straw under her back, heard the sounds of wind and bubbling river water mingling in her dazed ears as she felt the warmth of him all the way down the length of her tingling body.

It was only when she felt his fingers brushing lightly over her breast that her eyes flew open and she struggled briefly.

But he held her there with gentle firmness, controlled her with the weight of his body, one powerful leg thrown across hers to keep her from moving away.

"Let me," he said softly, holding her eyes as surely as he held her body, his fingers trespassing over her small, taut breasts as if they had every right in the world to be there.

"Don't," she pleaded in a choked whisper. Her wide, dark eyes pleaded with his blazing gray ones in a silence that magnified the sound of his fingers brushing over the cotton of her blouse.

"Why?" he asked.

"It's so intimate," she managed, hating the helpless reaction of her body that was telling him blatantly how much she was enjoying it.

He bent his blond head and brushed his mouth over her eyelids, forcing them shut. "Don't look at me with those accusing eyes," he whispered. "I'm not going to hurt you. I only want the feel of you, the softness of you under my hands. I want to show you how it can be between a man and a woman."

"You . . . you just want to humiliate me again, the way you did that day . . . in the barn," she choked.

She felt him grow taut before his mouth touched her cheek, her neck just below her ear. "That's not the reason," he whispered gruffly. "If you need one, it's because I'm starving for you, is that blunt enough?"

He lifted his head and she opened her eyes, watching the hard mouth poised over hers, feeling the banked tension in his body. "Don't...don't force me," she whispered apprehensively. "Don't . . . be rough."

"I'll cherish you, if you'll lie still and let me," he breathed against her mouth. "All you have to say is 'no,' darling." His heavy blond eyebrows drew together as his lips fitted themselves exactly to hers, pressing them gently apart. His big hands cupped her face, holding it just where he wanted it, while he kissed her as if he'd die trying to get enough of her soft, tremulous mouth. She found herself soothed by his controlled ardor. She relaxed against him, letting herself sink into the pine straw.

"You see?" he asked, lifting his mouth to brush it over her face in slow, soft kisses that lit a fire in her blood. "I'm not going to pounce on you."

"You know so much about women," she murmured, "and I know so little about men. We're hardly matched."

His lips tugged into a faint smile. He rested his weight on his elbow and studied her flushed face, her lazy, sensuous eyes. His gaze dropped to her blouse and he eased one finger under the edge of the neckline where it plunged into the narrow space between her small breasts.

He watched the helpless reaction in her eyes as he touched her bare flesh, easing his warm, faintly calloused fingers onto the soft, white swell under the wispy lace of her bra.

"You feel so exquisitely soft," he whispered, his fingers slow and gentle, edging toward the taut peak.

Her nails bit into his upper arms and her breath caught. Nothing in her life had been like this, no man had ever touched her this way—it was so different from that nightmare attack of her youth, so caring and tender.

She felt herself go taut, and strange tinglings made her body tremble with anticipation.

"Easy, darling," he whispered softly, leaning close to brush his mouth lightly against hers as his fingers moved again, gentling her. "This is part of it. I'm not going to hurt you. Just relax against me and let it happen."

Her eyes looked straight up into his. "King, this is...the first time..." she whispered brokenly, trying to tell him, to make him understand the devastating experience it was.

But he seemed to know it already, smiling down at her as he moved, placing his warm mouth over her lips, increasing the pressure gently as his hand eased down, and then up, swallowing her, and she cried out involuntarily at the unexpected surge of pleasure.

He caught his own breath at the wild little sound, drawing back a whisper to look at her. "Magic," he murmured gruffly. "What we do to each other is magic. Buds opening in the sun..."

She felt the violent shudder of his heart against her body, the rasp of his breath, as he kissed her again, deeply this time. She felt new sensations, wild, delicious surges of pleasure that worked their witchcraft on every tingling nerve. Her hands slid up his arms, feeling him, caressing him. They went around his neck and buried themselves in the thick, cool strands of his hair, to keep him close.

She was vaguely aware that both his hands were under her blouse, but she wasn't aware of what they were doing until she felt them against her bare skin, cupping her, molding her, rough and tender and warm, and her eyes flew open and looked straight up into his.

His tanned face looked strained, his eyes narrow and glittering as they read hers. "You fit my hands as if you'd been created for them," he said in a voice she didn't recognize.

She flushed, her lips parting on an unsteady breath.

He looked down at the blouse, under which his hands were outlined as he touched her. "I want to look at you, Teddi," he said quietly. "This isn't enough."

The thought of his eyes on her bareness was enough to bring her heart into her throat. She wanted that. The breeze on her skin, his eyes seeing her. She wanted him with a suddenness that startled her, all her untouched emotions roused to the point of pain as he caressed her.

"Frightened, little virgin?" he asked softly. "You know I won't hurt you."

"Oh, yes, I know," she said. She reached up and touched his face, daringly, her fingertips tracing the hard line of his mouth, his straight, arrogant nose, pushing back a shock of thick, sun-streaked hair from his broad forehead.

"Do you want it?" he asked quietly.

She touched his mouth, fascinated with it. "If I don't say no right now," she confessed honestly, "I won't be able to. You make me feel as if I'm burning up," she whispered.

"You make me feel the same way," he admitted, yielding reluctantly to the plea in her eyes. He drew his hands away from her body with a heavy sigh, and leaned them on either side of her head. His darkened eyes searched hers. "This is the first time for me, too, did you know?"

She smiled lazily, breathing more steadily now. "Pull the other one, Great White Rancher," she teased.

He grinned back, tugging at a lock of her short hair. "I'm serious. You're the first virgin I've made love to since I was sixteen. And this," he added wickedly, "is the first time in years that I've had to stop."

She searched his eyes, loving him, aching for more than just physical contact. She would have given anything for his love. She sighed. "I'm sorry."

"There's no need." He traced one of her thin eyebrows with a lazy finger. "Teddi, haven't you ever wanted a man?"

She swallowed. She was tempted to tell him all of it, nightmare and all, but this wasn't the time. It would spoil things between them. "No," she said after a minute. "At least, not before you."

He leaned his forehead against hers with a rough sigh. "Oh, honey, what a thing to admit to a man," he ground out. "Can't you tell how much I want you?"

It was hard to miss, as close as he was, and she felt faintly embarrassed by the knowledge. "I ... don't imagine you have this problem too often," she murmured.

He drew away and stared down at her as if he had immediate fears for her sanity, and she flushed beet-red.

"I mean," she corrected, avoiding his gaze, "I don't imagine that many women say 'no' to you."

"We won't talk about other women," he said firmly. "I'm not a playboy, if that's what you're insinuating."

"You'd hardly have time to be, the way you push yourself here at the ranch," she agreed, glancing up at him. "You work much too hard."

He toyed with a strand of her hair. "Habit, darling," he admitted, and the endearment sounded genuine. "I've always had to work hard. In the early days, if I'd allowed myself much time for recreation, everything we had would have gone on the auction block. I had mother and Jenna to think about after my father died, and three properties to manage. I had to keep everything going."

"And you've made a success of all of them," she said. Her fingers touched the silky hair at his temples. "It's made you hard, though."

"Business is ruthless, little one, didn't you know?"

"Yes, I know," she murmured, remembering her own hard knocks in the world of modeling when she'd first entered it.

"Your own life hasn't been easy," he remarked.

"It wasn't so bad, after I got to boarding school," she lied. A smile touched her mouth. "And I had Jenna to talk to."

His face seemed to harden. "When I wasn't making things difficult for you, you mean. I've been a brute to you at times. But you can't know the pressures I was under, the way it's been with me." His darkening eyes met her puzzled ones and dropped to her mouth. "Kiss me," he said gruffly, bending. "Kiss me the way you wanted to that morning in the stables when I teased you."

Without even thinking, she locked her hands behind his head and dragged it down to hers, letting her mouth tell him how hungry she'd been, and still was, holding him close, close....

"Don't you like to taste me?" he murmured against her mouth.

"I am," she murmured back.

He rubbed his nose against hers. "I'm going to have to teach you how to kiss, I can see that right now."

"I know how," she protested.

"Little girl kisses," he scoffed with a wicked gleam in his eyes. "Not half intimate enough. I like it like this, Teddi..." He caught her cheeks and teased her lips with his until they parted hungrily. His tongue shot past them, and she clutched him as he taught her things she'd never known about the way people kissed. He didn't just use his lips; she felt the gentle thrust of his tongue, the nibbling pressure of lips and teeth as he tormented her until she thought she'd go mad.

"Please, King," she whispered brokenly, her nails biting into his back, her eyes riveted to his mouth. "Please, please...!"

"No holding back this time," he growled as his mouth took hers fully. "Kiss me."

And she kissed him back as hungrily as a new wife, as passionately as a woman who'd just found the love of her life. With a sense of awe, she felt the full weight of his body settling over hers until they were locked together, breast to breast, thigh to thigh, hip to hip, and she clung as the unfamiliar contact burned the most exquisite sensations into her reeling mind.

"King," she whispered into his devouring mouth.

"Darling," he whispered back on a hard groan, shifting as he felt the soft, involuntary movement of her young body, surprising a sweet little cry from her throat.

She felt herself trembling. Incredibly, so was he, and even as she felt her body yielding everything he was demanding, he suddenly stiffened and, with a muffled curse, rolled away from her. He lay breathing roughly on his back, one knee drawn up between them, his forearms over his face.

"King...?" she asked, concerned at the rigidity of his big body.

"Go walk around for a minute, love," he said in a taut, aching tone, "and give me a little while to lie here and curse my own stupidity. Go on," he added when she hesitated.

She got up shakily and walked over to the bank of the river, watching it run lazily between the banks while her heartbeat slowly calmed. Her back against a tree at the edge, she tore off a bit of bark and sailed it down into the water, her eyes drifting from the majestic pines to the mountains beyond.

She felt rather than saw him behind her a little bit later, and she dropped her eyes to the ground.

"Embarrassed?" he asked gently as he lit a cigarette.

"A little," she admitted quietly. "I...didn't know, you see."

He laughed softly, drawing her close beside him with a protective arm around her shoulders. "We're both human," he murmured. "And together, we're volatile. I should have expected it."

She looked up at him shyly. "I wasn't teasing..."

"Don't you think I know that?" His eyes searched hers quietly. "It was beautiful. Not some sordid roll in the hay, not lust. I've never been that gentle with a woman in my life—or that intent on pleasing one. You're... very special, little one," he added, frowning. "You make me vulnerable in ways I couldn't have imagined."

She dropped her eyes to his chest, drinking in the sound of his deep, tender voice, the words that revealed he had some kind of feeling for her, after all.

"I thought it was the other way around," she whispered.

His mouth brushed against her forehead. "You can't imagine what it did to me," he breathed, "touching you that way, knowing that no other man ever had." He caught his breath and hugged her close for an instant before he let her go and moved away to retrieve his hat from the ground, where it had fallen an eternity ago.

"As much as I hate the thought," he said, "I'm a working man. And to make it all worse, I've got that bloody accountant coming this afternoon." His eyes darted to catch hers and he looked faintly irritated. "There's something you need to know about him before he gets here."

"What?" she asked, smiling.

He stared at her, captivated by the radiance of her face. "No," he said. "Not yet. I'll tell you later. Come on, tiger, let's go home."

The ride back was quiet, and Teddi didn't admit to herself how much she was hoping that when he helped her down in the stables, he'd kiss her just once more. But when they reached the huge barn where the horses were quartered, Blakely and Jenna were just coming from the house, and Teddi felt her heart sink.

"There you are," Jenna said, clinging to Blakely's hand and laughing as if she had the sun captured inside her. "Some man is here to see you, King. Mother drove into Calgary to pick him up, and they've just come back."

King nodded. "The accountant," he said with a strangely secretive glance at Teddi. "Well, let's go in. You might as well all be introduced at once. He's going to be here for a few days."

Teddi dismounted by herself and fell into step with Jenna and Blakely while one of the ranch hands took the horses away. None of them could keep up with King's long strides; he was walking like a man with a distasteful goal ahead.

"Here's King, now," Mary was saying as they walked into the living room.

The visitor stood up, lean and dark and brown-haired, smiling crookedly when he saw Teddi. She got a good look at him at the same time, and all the bad luck in the world seemed to descend on her at once. This wasn't just any accountant. This was Bruce Billingsly, who'd hounded her so single-mindedly at the beginning of the year that she'd even risked King's contempt and accepted an invitation from Jenna at Easter. Bruce, who wouldn't take no for an answer.

So now she knew who King's secret informant was, who'd been telling him lies about her life, her work. She knew who'd helped to poison his mind against her. And here was the culprit in person, with a gleam in his eye telling her clearly that he had more mischief in mind.

Her wary eyes turned to King, who was watching the silent exchange with a cold scrutiny.

"Small world, Teddi," Bruce laughed, moving close to bend and kiss her on the cheek, to her amazed indignation. "How do you do, Miss Devereaux, Blakely? Good to see you again, King, but," he added, with a raised eyebrow as he drew a rigid Teddi to his side, "what's my girl doing here?"

Chapter Seven

There was a small flash of emotion in King's gray eyes that no one seemed to catch except Teddi. When he turned to Bruce Billingsly, there was nothing in his expression except a trace of mockery.

"As I told you before," he told Teddi over Bruce's shoulder, "we have a mutual acquaintance."

"Sure. Me," Bruce said with a grin. "Oh, I've been singing your praises for the past several months, honey. King didn't know much about your modeling career, but I filled him in."

I'll just bet you did, Teddi thought miserably, remembering how she'd tried to elude her aunt's boyfriend. He was like so many of Dilly's other pickups, arrogant, a little conceited, and money-hungry as well. Since he couldn't land Dilly, he'd set his sights on

Teddi, with a lot of enthusiasm and no success at all. And apparently when he realized that King had a passing acquaintance with her, he decided to make sure that nothing could develop in that quarter while he was pursuing her. He'd even shown up at college once or twice, and she'd had a time trying to shoo him away.

Teddi's apprehensive eyes looked up into King's and read the disgust and contempt there. Bruce's arrival had killed the trust that had been growing so delicately between them. The beautiful morning would become a memory, there would never be a repeat of it. She saw that in King's hard face. It was as if he'd been looking for an excuse, a weapon. And now he had it.

"Aren't you glad to see me, Teddi?" Bruce, grinning, hugged her.

King stabbed his hands into his jean pockets. "You didn't tell me about your budding romance, darling," he said, and it didn't sound like an endearment anymore. "But now that Billingsly is here, perhaps you'll have time to pursue it. When," he added with a cold smile for Bruce, "he's through getting my books in order. And there's no time like the present. Shall we get to it?"

"But, King, he's only just arrived," Mary protested, her sense of hospitality outraged.

"He didn't come here for a social gathering, Mother," he reminded her. "Billingsly?"

Bruce knew the whip in that deep voice, apparently. "I'm ready," he lied, letting go of Teddi reluctantly. "I'll see you later, honey, we've got a lot to talk about."

"Indeed we have," Teddi said with a venomous smile, her dark eyes flashing.

King didn't even look her way, and his back was arrow-straight as he led the shorter man out of the room.

"What was that all about?" Jenna asked, while Blakely and her mother discussed ranch business.

"I told you about him," Teddi moaned. "The one who chased me until I couldn't stay in New York at all for being hounded?"

"That's him?" Jenna gasped. "Here?"

"Here, though heaven only knows how. He works for the firm that does King's accounting, I suppose," she said miserably. "Now that I think of it, he told me he knew King when he was running after me, but I never asked how. I should have realized . . ."

"That's the man who came up to college looking for you," Jenna burst out, remembering. "Holy mackerel!"

"He just wouldn't take no for an answer. I thought that when I came up here at Easter I'd finally gotten rid of him," she said with a wan smile. "Oh, Jenna, what am I going to do? King believes him, he really believes there's something between us. I couldn't even push the silly man away, I was too shocked at seeing him here, and heaven only knows what lies he's been telling King about me! And King will believe every word," she added miserably.

Jenna was beginning to add things up. The look on Teddi's face when she and King had ridden in, the very tender light in her brother's eyes, the slight swell of Teddi's lower lip, the pine straw in her hair—it all began to make sense.

"Just what were you and King doing in the woods besides discussing international economics and the future of democracy?" Jenna asked, tongue in cheek.

Teddi blushed, and Jenna had the answer she wanted. She laughed delightedly.

"Now I know why King's been so hard to live with," she murmured. "Mother said he'd been horrible since Easter. Something happened then, too, didn't it, after you threw that feed bucket at him? Oh, my friend—" her gray eyes lit up "—if you knew how I've dreamed of having you for a sister-in-law...."

"It isn't like that," Teddi protested, embarrassed. "And you mustn't say anything. Oh, please, Jenna, you can't!"

There was a long, heartfelt sigh. "All right," came the grudging promise, "I'll keep quiet. But you do care for him, don't you?"

The dark eyes fell. "Yes," she admitted quietly. If caring could be described as a passionate obsession that hadn't waned in almost six years, then, yes, it was definitely caring.

"And King?" Jenna prodded.

She shrugged. "Who knows what he thinks? It doesn't matter now, anyway. He's always believed the worst of me, and now here's Bruce to feed him some of the most delicious lies he's ever tasted. He'll be overjoyed."

"Stop that," Jenna said sternly. "If King feels something for you himself, what makes you think he's going to believe Bruce? He's intelligent enough to know pique and hurt masculine pride when he sees them. If Bruce is just out for revenge, he'll see that, too."

"Will he?" Teddi said and shrugged. "Let's go and make some sandwiches. I imagine we'll have hungry mouths to feed any minute."

"Might as well, I suppose." Jenna looked worriedly toward Blakely and her mother. "Oh, Mother, we're going to make lunch!"

"Can I help?" Mary offered.

"No, dear, you talk to Blakely," Jenna encouraged, with a pointed look at Blakely, who reddened slightly. "It will only take a few minutes."

"What's going on back there?" Teddi whispered when they were out of earshot.

Jenna took a deep breath. "Blakely's going to ask her advice about how to deal with King. He...he wants to marry me," she added, faltering. Her eyes closed blissfully. "Teddi, he wants to marry me!" She looked as if she had every single blessing in the world as she said it.

If Teddi had any doubts about her friend's emotional involvement with Blakely, that settled them.

"Can I help?" she asked her friend.

"I may have to call on every single friend I have in the world and all my acquaintances to get around King," Jenna said miserably. "He'll say I'm too young, that Blakely won't be able to give me what I want, that I won't settle..."

All of which was just what King had told Teddi, and she had to look away to keep her best friend from reading it in her expressive face.

"I love him," Jenna said stubbornly. "If I have to draw water from a well and make my own clothes, I'll do it, as long as I can live with him. That's all I want in the world. And I'll get it," she added with a stubborn set to her jaw. "You just watch me!"

"I believe you," Teddi assured her with a laugh. She was a lot like King, and if anybody had a chance of holding out against him, it was Jenna.

The men ate their sandwiches in the study, so Teddi was spared a confrontation. But when they sat down to dinner that night, it was as close to civilized warfare as Teddi had ever come.

Bruce sat across from her, his eyes resting appreciatively on the soft white shirtwaist dress she'd donned. King glared at her from the head of the table, his eyes as cold as winter. She felt like a human sacrifice, and Jenna's evident amusement didn't help a bit. Mary, blissfully oblivious of the undercurrents around her, chatted enthusiastically about an upcoming art exhibit in Calgary.

"I thought you'd be working this summer, Teddi," Bruce murmured when there was a pause in the conversation. "I asked for a local assignment in New York for that reason."

Teddi met his eyes coolly. "Did you?" she muttered, hating him for what he'd done to her fragile relationship with King. "I thought I'd made it quite clear that I didn't have time for a lot of night life."

"Pull the other one, honey," he laughed, his eyes calculating as he measured King's interest. "I've seen you in nightclubs all over New York."

Teddi's eyes dilated. "You most certainly have not!" she cried.

"Sure, if that's the way you want it," he agreed, making it sound as if he was covering up for her. "It doesn't matter, you know," he added in a demoralized tone. "I know I couldn't compete with the kind of money your escorts had. I'm just a working man."

Teddi's fingers clenched on her fork, and just for one wild second, she contemplated the effect of throwing her plate across the table at him. His eyes were laughing at her. He knew what he was doing, and she realized all at once that her first impression had been right. He was going to crucify her for the blow she'd dealt his masculine pride. If he couldn't have her, no other man was going to, especially not King.

"I don't need to date rich men," she bit off.

"You don't?" Bruce asked innocently. "But, sweet, Dilly doesn't give you a penny toward your education. You've got to get money somewhere."

He was planting deadly seeds and finding fertile ground in King's already suspicious mind.

"I make enough to support myself," Teddi said.

"You must, if you can take the whole summer off for a vacation," Bruce said with an insinuating look toward King. "Or are you up here on a 'fishing' trip?"

King's expression was one of pure fury.

With a mighty effort, Teddi lifted her coffee cup to her lips and managed not to burst into tears. It was like having an invisible knife take the skin off an inch at a time, and nobody could see the wounds. Especially not King, who got to his feet and tossed his napkin down.

"If you're through, Billingsly?" he asked with maddening carelessness, leading the way out of the dining room.

Teddi watched him go, aware of Bruce's triumphant smile as he followed. The light went out of her eyes, her soul, at that moment, because she knew King had believed Bruce. All that she had kept from him was suddenly out in the open. Now King knew that she was responsible for her own educational expenses, her living expenses, that Dilly didn't help out—and he believed one more thing, that she needed money. He would inevitably come to the conclusion that she had been trying to trap him, especially since she'd come to Gray Stag instead of going back to New York during summer vacation. He would fit those puzzle pieces together, along with what Bruce had let drop about her so-called "dates" with wealthy men—a lie if there ever was one—and her indifference to working men. And when he put all that together, he was going to have a false picture of a penniless young woman out to catch a wealthy man any way she could. The fact that she flirted with him at Easter would take on new meaning. And there was nothing, absolutely nothing she could do to convince him that he was wrong, because now he'd think she was a liar. Chances were good that he'd also doubt her innocence, think it was part of the act, part of her plan to trap him into marriage. She felt tears welling up in her eyes.

"Coffee's hot!" she said as she put her cup down with a laugh, hoping to explain her sudden tears.

"Suppose we take the pot in there," Jenna suggested icily, "and pour it over Mr. Billingsly's head? What a bunch of rot! And my big, dumb brother sitting there looking as if he believed every word! Men are the stupidest . . . !"

"What an excellent suggestion," Mary said, her usually kind face drawn into taut lines. "And I'll have the daily maid put him in the green guest room. It has the lumpy mattress, remember?" she added with a malicious smile.

"Mother, you're a jewel." Jenna grinned.

"I think I'll go look for a few rocks to tuck in among the lumps," Teddi said with a wan smile. "See you later."

She walked out, a slim, dejected figure, and two pairs of pained, sympathetic eyes followed her.

She was expecting King to confront her, and minutes later he found her in the moonlit garden behind the house and paused just in front of her.

"Bruce told me what good friends you two were," he mocked. His darkening gray eyes cut at her as he spoke. "I never knew until today whether to believe him."

"But this evening's performance convinced you," she replied.

"I beg your pardon?"

"Never mind," she said, turning dejectedly away. "Naturally you believed every word he said, it only confirmed your own sterling opinion of me."

"Aren't you going to deny it?" he challenged.

"No," she replied stiffly. "I can't see that it makes that much difference."

He stared at her small, stiff back, his eyes doubtful, uncertain. But she didn't turn, and she missed the expression that crossed his hard face.

"Think how fortunate you were to have been saved from me in the nick of time," she said over her shoulder as she started toward the house. "Good old Bruce, he's a knight, he is."

"How much of that innocence was an act?" he asked coldly.

She'd known that question would come, and she was ready for it. If he wanted to believe lies, she'd give him some more, the beast! "All of it, darling," she taunted, batting her eyelashes at him, while her heart splintered in her chest. "That's what you believe, isn't it, and Kingston Devereaux never makes mistakes about women," she reminded him, using his own words.

She walked away and left him standing there. What good would it have done to contradict Bruce, anyway? She consoled herself. The morning had only been a dream.

In the days that followed, Bruce dogged her every step. The only good thing about it was that King kept his nose to the grindstone, with a single-mindedness that raised Jenna's pale eyebrows.

The time inevitably came when she and Bruce confronted each other, unexpectedly one morning when Jenna and Blakely had invited Teddi to go for a swim. She'd rushed to get away from Bruce's hot eyes and King's cold ones, hurriedly donning her pale yellow two-piece suit and throwing a sundress over it.

A long whistle met her as she came down the staircase to find Bruce lounging against the study door, watching her.

"You get lovelier by the day," he told her. "Teddi, when are you going to stop avoiding me?"

"Never," she told him bluntly. "Look, I don't want to hurt your feelings, but I've told you until I'm blue in the face that I don't feel that way about you! Why can't you just leave me alone?"

"Because I learned young that a man can get anything he wants if he keeps after it long enough," he replied confidently.

"Not people," she replied. "Not ever people. You can't force people to love, Bruce."

The grin widened. "Who's talking about love?" he murmured, eyeing her body.

She stiffened. "I'm not ready for that kind of relationship with any man."

"So you said," he murmured, "but there's fire under all that ice, I'd bet my right arm on it. I could make you change your mind. There's never been a woman I couldn't get," he added with hateful confidence.

"Meet number one," she hurled back, tired of arguing. "I don't want you. Can't you get that through your thick skull!"

"Who do you want, the cattle baron?" he growled. "It won't work, Teddi, I'm not handing you over to him without a fight. I saw you first."

"What are you talking about?"

"I've told King things about you," he said huskily. "None of it very flattering, but he believed it. I can make it even worse if you don't play ball. You're my girl, and I'm not giving you up."

"Look, will you just leave me alone?" she burst out, feeling her control snap.

"I can't," he murmured. His eyes leered at her. "You're a knockout, do you know? You drive me wild," he concluded, and his desire found expression in his eyes as he moved forward. He caught her before she could react and dragged her into his arms, emotion clouding his eyes as he forced her to be still, despite her struggles.

"Turn me loose," she ground out, trying to find enough space to kick his shin.

"Not on your life," he grumbled, bruising her with his tight hold. "You threw me over at Easter. You tore my pride to shreds. Wouldn't even let me get close, give me a chance to get to know you. Well, here I am and here you are, and this time you're going to spend some time with me or I'll ruin you with your rich friends. I didn't have old Mr. Murray send me out here to do King's books for nothing..."

"Think so?" she asked. She dipped suddenly and brought her foot down sharply on his instep.

He cried out, and she tore away from him, breathing hard, her hair and eyes wild.

It was at that moment that King came in the door. His sharp eyes went from Teddi's disheveled appearance to his accountant's pained expression. Immediately, he jumped to his own conclusions.

"I'll remind you that you're working on my time," King told Bruce with barely controlled anger. "That doesn't allow you the luxury of flirting with Teddi. Clear?"

Bruce shrugged, shooting a lightning glance at Teddi. "Whatever you say, Mr. Devereaux. My fault. I shouldn't have let myself be tempted," he added damningly as he turned and went back into the study.

"Leave him alone," King told her coldly, his eyes contemptuous as they ran the length of her body. "I should have followed my instincts and let you go to New York in the first place. We're a small community here, with old-fashioned moral values. If I catch you playing around with your boyfriend under my roof, you'll both go out on your ears."

And before she could voice the furious reply her mind was forming, he followed Bruce into the study and slammed the door in her face.

Minutes later, she was fuming in the cold, clear water of the river.

"King again?" Jenna asked as soon as Blakely left them to dress in the secluded shade of some nearby bushes.

"However did you guess?" Teddi asked with a weary sigh.

"Oh, I'm getting quite good at mind reading," came the amused reply. "He's giving you a rough time about Bruce, huh? The idiot. He's just impossible lately. Ever since Bruce came, in fact." She glanced at Teddi. "Doesn't he act jealous, though?" she mused.

Teddi's face was suffused with color. "King? Jealous of me?"

"Why don't you tell him the truth?" Jenna asked as they climbed out of the water. She paused and turned to face her friend. "Teddi, what have you got to lose?"

"My self-respect, my pride, my—"

"You can do without those. But can you do without King?"

Teddi let her eyes drop to the ground, where the sun shining through the leaves was making shadow patterns. "I've done very well without him for almost six years," she murmured.

"He feels something," Jenna said quietly. "We both know that. But unless you make him see the truth, he's very likely to wall his emotions up for good where you're concerned."

That was possible. And he had felt something, Teddi knew that better than her friend did, remembering the hunger of his hard mouth, the urgency of his body against hers that magic morning in the woods. King had dashed her pride to slivers once—could she take it if he did that again? On the other hand, no one achieved anything worthwhile without courage. There were no great rewards without great risks.

She took a deep breath. "Well, I can't look any worse in his eyes than I already do, can I?" she asked with a whimsical smile.

"He was going out to check the stock this morning after he finished with Bruce," Jenna murmured. "You might find him in the stables."

"What a smelly place to chase a man," Teddi grumbled.

"At least it's private," Jenna laughed. "Uh, Blakely and I discovered that early on. Now, get out there and fight. Just remember one thing—you catch more flies with honey than you can with vinegar."

Teddi sighed. "There's just one thing wrong with that philosophy."

"What's that?"

Teddi gave her a mischievous glance. "Who's going to hold King while I smear honey on him?"

Jenna simply threw up her hands.

The walk to the stables was the longest Teddi ever remembered making. Several times she almost decided to turn and go back to the house. The "what ifs" drove her wild. What if he didn't believe her? What if she told him how much she loved him, and he laughed at her? What if she threw her arms around him, and he pushed her away? It was insane, this idea of Jenna's. She felt a sense of foreboding. There was still time, she could turn back. But what if she did, and King turned away from her forever?

Resolutely she forced herself not to worry about her still-damp hair, about her bareness under the sundress. In her haste, she had thrown on the dress, leaving her wet bathing suit with Jenna.

She entered the dimly lit barn, blinking her eyes to adjust them to the darkness inside. Her gaze lit on a shadow that moved into view out of one of the neat hay-filled stalls.

It was King, denim-clad and powerful looking, and as unyielding as the walls.

"Looking for your lover?" he asked in a mocking tone.

"No, actually I was looking for you," she said before her courage deserted her.

He lifted his head, looking down at her with his lips slightly pursed, studying her slender young body, which was only barely covered by the yellow-and-white gingham dress. It was a seductive little coverup, held over her breasts by a narrow band of elastic, elasticized at the waist, barely brushing her knees at the hem. Her feet were encased in strappy little white sandals. The picture she made was one of sunny innocence, joyful youth.

A glimmer of passion appeared in King's hard face as he looked at her, and that tiny chink in his armor gave her enough nerve to approach him. He wasn't indifferent to her, that was certain enough. And all her small doubts were instantly erased when she pressed her hands against his damp shirt front and moved close. His heart was beating too hard, his broad chest rising and falling much too rapidly for a calm man. The tautness of his body gave her answers to questions she wouldn't have dared ask.

"Now will you listen to me?" she asked, looking up into darkening, stormy eyes. Her hands flattened against his shirt, faintly caressing. "Bruce is just getting even with me. Earlier this year, he wanted to date me and I wouldn't go out with him. It hurt his pride, and now he's out for revenge. I don't want Bruce. I...I want you, King," she breathed, going on tiptoe to brush her lips against his throat, his chin, the corner of his mouth. Bold with new confidence, feeling for the first time like a whole woman instead of a frightened girl, she reached up to lock her fingers in his thick hair and pressed her hungry lips against his hard, unyielding mouth.

"Oh, kiss me," she breathed achingly, pressing closer to his hard, taut body with a hunger that flared like a match thrown into dry wood. "Kiss me!"

Steely fingers suddenly bit into her arms and tore loose her grip on him. He thrust her from him with a force that almost tripped her. She caught her balance, staring at him with wide, apprehensive eyes.

"Don't you ever," he said in a voice like a razor's edge, "try that with me again! My God, everything he said about you was the truth, wasn't it?" His accusing eyes swept over her. "This is the real you, isn't it, darling? Eager, willing, wanton... and there I was, treating you like porcelain because I didn't want to frighten you. Frighten you! How much do you get for a night, Teddi?" he asked with a half smile that sickened her. "Maybe we can work something out."

Devastated, she wrapped her arms around her trembling body and turned to leave.

"No comeback?" he taunted. "What's the matter, are you holding out for a ring? No chance, honey. You'll have to ply your wiles on some other rich rancher. I just went off the market!"

She turned at the entrance to the barn and looked back at him. "First blood to you, Mr. Devereaux," she said with cool pride. "You're wrong about me. You always have been. You'll believe anything you're told, as long as it's something bad, won't you? Well, I'm no more a hooker than you are a gentleman, and someday you'll find that out. Not that it will make any difference to me. Rich or not, I want no part of a man who's morally blind.''

And she turned and walked away.

King didn't come in for dinner that night, and Teddi pleaded a splitting headache and stayed in her room that night. The headache was real enough, she told herself—six foot three with blond hair and gray eyes and the farsightedness of a mole.

She'd just pulled on a long yellow cotton nightgown when there was a knock at her door.

She stared at it blankly. ''Who's there?''

There was no answer. Maybe... she brightened. Maybe it was King; maybe he'd had second thoughts and had finally decided to listen. She went to the door and pulled it open. Bruce, in his pajamas and robe, stood outside grinning at her.

She tried to shut the door, but he wouldn't let her. He forced her back into the room, leaving the door carefully open, like a man with a master plan who wouldn't brook interference.

''What do you think you're doing?'' she cried, struggling with him as he forced her back against the bed.

''It's called the coup de grace, darling,'' he said in an undertone, abruptly pushing her back onto the bedcovers just before he threw himself down beside her and buried his face in her throat. "Guess who's coming up the stairs?"

She pushed futilely at him, barely avoiding his hot mouth as it went across her cheek and tried to catch her lips.

She cringed when she heard the door suddenly open even farther. Turning her head, she saw King standing in the doorway, watching with condemning eyes.

Bruce sat up and ran a hand through his disheveled hair, grinning at King.

"Sorry about that," he told his employer. "We got carried away and forgot to close the door."

King glanced from the younger man, clad only in a robe, to Teddi dressed in the semisheer cotton nightgown. The contempt in his face was unbearable.

"I'll expect you both to be packed and out of here by tomorrow morning," King said in a quiet, very controlled tone.

Bruce gaped at him, as if he hadn't expected anything so drastic. "But, King . . . Mr. Devereaux . . . what will I tell my firm?"

"That's your affair," King said coldly. "I'll let you explain it after I've given them the bare facts and requested another accountant. I warned you about playing around under my roof. You might have listened."

"But—!" Bruce cut short his protest when the door slammed shut.

He stared at it, bug-eyed. "He didn't mean that, surely!"

"Of course he meant it," Teddi said numbly. She got off the bed and tugged on her thick toweling robe. She felt her world ending with a sense of quiet inevitability.

"I didn't think he'd react like that," Bruce choked out. "I just wanted to make sure he didn't snap you up before I had one more chance, that's all."

"Snap me up." Teddi laughed bitterly, shoving her hands in the deep pockets of her robe. "He's hated me for five years. He's always believed I was some sort of nymphomaniac. You only confirmed his darkest suspicions. But it backfired, didn't it?"

He sighed wearily. "I feel sick," he mumbled. "I've got car payments, my rent's due...and when the firm finds out I've been sent back, I may lose my job."

"I'm sorry," she said, "but you did bring it on yourself. I told you how I felt. You just wouldn't listen. Would you please go?"

He looked up, noticing for the first time the tears running down her pale cheeks, the horrible expression in her eyes. "You love him," he said with dawning realization.

She hunched her drooped shoulders. "I had a tiny chance before you came. Now there's no chance at all. I hope life is as empty for you as you've just made it for me," she added with a flash of spirit.

He seemed to shrink before her eyes. "If it's any consolation, I feel like a prize idiot. I meant to upset the cart, any way I could, because I wanted you to notice me. I couldn't compete with King—who could?

And the way he looked at you . . . well, I thought if I could get the competition out of the way, I might still have a chance." He met her eyes, and there was a sadness in his. "I've never felt this way about a woman. You were like an obsession." He sighed. "At any rate, I am sorry, for what good it does."

"Not very much, I'm afraid," she said honestly.

"As I thought. Well...good night. I'll see you in the morning. Perhaps if I explained to King . . . ?"

She smiled sadly. "He wouldn't listen," she replied. "When he makes up his mind, that's it."

"I really am sorry," he added just before he left the room.

But she didn't reply. What else was there to say?

It was late before she finally got to sleep, and she dragged out of bed the next morning with eyes that were red from the combination of tears and insomnia. She packed before she went downstairs, knowing that King had meant every word of that terse command the night before.

She went into the dining room at the usual time for breakfast, expecting and hoping to see King already gone. But he was sitting at the table by himself, a cup of coffee in front of him, and nothing else.

She moved into the room with a bravado she didn't feel, elegant in her white pleated skirt, white gauze blouse and black bolero jacket.

"Could I have a cup of coffee?" she asked, intimidated by the expression on his hard face, the glittering anger in his deep-set eyes. He was wearing brown denims with a pullover beige shirt, and despite his fair hair, he looked dark and foreboding.

"Help yourself, darling," he said coldly.

She sat down as far away from him as she could get and poured herself a cup of black coffee from the pot on the warmer. The mahogany dining table was long, and she felt uncomfortable seated at one end in her brocade-upholstered chair. She glanced from the crystal prisms of the chandelier to King, silhouetted against the drawn pale-jade curtains at the window behind him.

"Is . . . is Jenna coming down?" she asked falteringly.

"She and mother have already been down," he said curtly. "I asked them to stay upstairs until you left. I've told my sister that if she continues her friendship with you, I'll send her young Blakely to the Australian property for an indefinite stay."

The pure chauvinism of the remark made her bristle. "In chains?" she asked with a cool smile. "Or perhaps you thought you'd make him swim the Pacific while you rowed alongside yelling suggestions?"

His face went harder. "My family's business is no longer any of your concern," he said remotely. "Your friend should be down any minute. I've lent him a vehicle to drive you into Calgary. I'll have it picked up later."

She stared into her coffee, too drained of emotion to even cry. Not only was she losing King, but Jenna was to be forbidden any contact with her. Her only friend....

"Do you have enough money to get to New York?" he asked with casual politeness.

"Yes," she bit off.

He finished his coffee and set the cup down firmly. "How is he in bed?" he asked, lashing out unexpectedly.

Her eyes jerked up and she glared at him, with pain and anger in every line of her pale face. "Just great, thanks!" she threw at him. "He could give you lessons!"

"You little tramp!" he breathed. He was on his feet before she could move, reaching down to drag her out of the chair and up into his hard arms.

"Put me down!" she cried, fighting. But he was strong—much stronger than Bruce had been. He carried her, squirming, into his study and kicked the door shut behind them without even breaking stride.

He threw her down onto the long, leather sofa and stood over her, breathing roughly, his face livid with barely leashed fury.

He paused just long enough to rip off the knit shirt, baring a chest with bronzed muscles under a thick wedge of curling dark blond hair, before he came down beside her.

"Go ahead, darling, fight me," he ground out, controlling her struggles easily as his mouth crushed down on hers. "It'll just make it that much more intense when I make you submit."

She felt his hands on her body, careless of hurting her, while she tried vainly to push him away, to free herself. She loved him, but what he was doing to her was monstrous. Her mind reeled back to that long-ago night, to the feel of that drunken beast's cruel hands, the hot searching of his mouth. She cried out, but King didn't seem to hear.

He dragged her blouse away from her skirt, and his hands went roughly under it, easily disposing of the lacy obstacles, to find her bare, soft flesh with rough fingers.

It was just like that long-ago night, and she was fighting suddenly for all she was worth, mindlessly fighting in a blind fury, sobbing, crying, her face contorted into a mask of panic-stricken terror.

His hands were busy again, on the buttons of her blouse, and before she could stop him, the fabric was suddenly out of the way, and King drew back. He held her by the wrists, his eyes cloudy as he studied her writhing body, her white face, her wide, frightened eyes.

He stood poised there, like a man barely able to think at all, staring down at her half-nude body, bare from the waist up where her blouse was pushed aside. For an instant, his gaze was riveted to the soft mounds of her breasts and he dragged in breaths like a man dying of oxygen deprivation. Did she imagine it, or was there a softening in his face, did his steely fingers relax just a little where they were biting into her wrists?

"Please," she whispered brokenly. "Please, King, don't hurt me!"

Something snapped in him at the husky sob of her voice. He looked back up at her face, and she watched the conflicting emotions war in his eyes.

"Teddi?" he murmured, seeming to snap back to sanity as he realized how frightened she was.

He let her go all at once and watched, frozen, as she dragged her blouse around herself and huddled into the corner of the sofa, crying like a terrified child in the dark, in little breathless, broken sobs that echoed through the room.

"I wouldn't have forced you," he managed tautly, his eyes never leaving her. "Must you have hysterics every time I touch you?"

"I was fourteen," she said in a strangled voice. "Dilly was going with a decorator who...who took a fancy to me. One night they had a terrible argument and she...she stormed out of the apartment and didn't come back. He'd been drinking, and I thought I'd be safer if I went to my room." She laughed brokenly, avoiding his eyes. "I almost made it. He caught me at the door and dragged me back to the couch and tore half my clothes off." Her eyes closed and she cringed. "He was like a wild animal. He hurt me terribly...hands all over me, horrible wet kisses...and just before he tried to force me, he heard Dilly at the door." She shivered at the memory. She couldn't even look at King. It would have been a revelation to her if she had, because his features had taken on the look of a man being dragged apart by a team of horses.

She swallowed. "He thought he was irresistible, you see, and it made him angry that I fought. He slapped me around quite a lot, and then dared me to tell Dilly. She didn't even question the marks on me," she added with a bitter smile.

She managed to fasten her blouse in the silence that followed. "I've never slept with Bruce," she said finally. "I've never slept with any man. Just the thought of it…terrifies me. I…I thought for a little while that I might be able to accept more than kisses…with you, at least," she whispered. "But not anymore." She stood up, turning toward the door.

"That was why you were so frightened of me in the car on the way back from Banff," he said quietly.

"Yes," she told him. "I…I suppose the scars go pretty deep. He was…quite brutal."

"Teddi!"

She paused with her hand on the doorknob, but she couldn't look at him. "I'll go with Bruce," she said with gentle pride. "And if you still want me to keep away from Jenna, I will."

"Oh, God, don't turn the knife!" he said in a barely audible tone. He started toward her, but she opened the door and moved quickly away from him.

He flinched. "I won't hurt you," he said, hesitating.

"So you promised me once before," she reminded him, choking on the word. "I think I'd die if you

touched me again. Please... all I want is to get away
from you!''

She turned, oblivious of the look on his face, and
ran all the way upstairs to her room. She didn't leave
it until she heard Jenna's concerned voice on the other
side. She opened the door and ran straight into her
friend's outstretched arms.

Chapter Eight

The only good thing about Teddi's abrupt arrival in New York was that Dilly was still away. There was a curt little note on the coffee table telling her that her aunt would most likely be away until late September.

Teddi called her agency first thing, and was pleased to hear that they had work for her right away.

"Velvet Moth is having a showing Saturday for buyers and the press," Mandy burst out enthusiastically. "I told Mr. Sethwick that you were out of town, but he insisted that he only wanted you to do his new gown. He calls it the 'firemist special,'" she added, teasing. "If you accept, you'll need a fitting at Jomar's in the morning at ten. And Lovewear wants a girl for a millinery ad, if you're interested in a go see. There's an open call Thursday morning at nine, there.

I've got a weather permitting for a soft drink commercial as well—you'd fit the client's requirements very well."

A weather permitting assignment would mean a cancellation fee if it fell through, and Teddi jumped at it. It would mean more exposure, too. But she was cautious.

"Who's shooting it?" she asked quickly before she accepted.

"Ronnie, remember him?" came the laughing reply from her agent.

"As long as it's not that crazy Irishman," Teddi said with a relieved sigh. "Do you remember, he made me jump the wall in that hosiery commercial he was shooting no less than fifty times? I was a nervous wreck when we finished, and it cost me twelve pair of hose because of the snags!"

"I hear he's given up fashion photography and gone into films," Mandy told her.

"And next thing," Teddi murmured, "we'll hear about a film producer going bankrupt on retakes."

Mandy giggled. "No doubt. Well, I'll get back to you on the commercial, and keep in touch tomorrow. Welcome back, by the way. How was Canada?"

"Cold," Teddi said without further ado, and hung up.

The next few days went by in a flash. She made sure that she didn't have time to think about King. Mandy outdid herself in bookings. Teddi did two commercials, the Velvet Moth fashion show, a photography session for the millinery ad and three photographic sessions for other ads. By the end of the week, she was exhausted. She spent Sunday with her feet in a hot tub of water and counted her blessings. She'd made enough to pay next semester's fees and would have just enough left over when all the checks came to pay her airfare back to school.

The slump season in the fashion industry was just down the road, but if she worked a little harder, she might save up a nest egg to carry her through the rest of the year. And the restaurant job near the college would keep her in clothes and incidentals.

That night, her dreams were wild and disturbed and full of King. She woke up at four in the morning crying, and got up to make coffee. Would she ever forget his cruelty to her, the cheap way he'd treated her? Would she ever stop thinking about the way it had been that morning they went riding, when, for the first time, she wasn't afraid, when she was able to give, to open her heart, to love him?

She got dressed in slacks and a loose white blouse with high-heeled sandals and waited impatiently for the agency to open so that she could call Mandy and see if there were any jobs for her. She took a long time over her makeup, did her nails carefully, packed her carryall with the essentials of her trade—brush, comb, makeup, tissues, shoes, hairpieces and clothes, anything she might need during a shooting—and wandered around the living room of the apartment to watch the sun rise over the sleeping city.

Why, oh, why did King always have to think the worst of her? She still cringed at the memory of his hands hurting her, his eyes contemptuous as they stared down at her bareness. It hadn't all been contempt, she reminded herself. For an instant he had seemed to be awed by her, savagely hungry for the sight and feel of her. Of course, any man could feel desire in those circumstances, it meant nothing. The thing that puzzled her was his unreasonable anger about Bruce. Jealousy would explain such fury, but King wasn't jealous of her, how could he be when he thought so little of her? But...why had he fired Bruce? Since his contempt was mainly for her, why punish a man he thought she'd tempted?

She sipped her lukewarm coffee with a grimace of distaste. How hard it was to kill hope, she thought miserably. All the way to the airport, with Bruce contrite and worried beside her, she'd hoped against hope that King would come after her. But he hadn't. She hadn't seen him again, after she left the study. When she'd gone downstairs, leaving Jenna behind, Bruce had been waiting, quiet and subdued, and King hadn't even **stay**ed around long enough to say good-bye.

Even the first few days she'd been home, she wondered if King might call. But he hadn't. Why should he? she asked herself, laughing aloud at her own idiocy. He didn't care. If he felt anything now, it was probably guilt over his treatment of her—if his hatred would permit that. At least now that he knew the truth, perhaps he thought less harshly of her.

King. Her eyes pictured him and closed on a new wave of tears. Would she ever get used to being apart from him? Every day she lived was filled with that kind of loneliness that only those who love in vain understand. It had always been King, from the time she was fifteen and got her first look at him. There'd been boys she dated, but none of them could hold her interest. King was so much a man, so far removed from ordinary men. Now she couldn't settle for less.

Angrily, she dashed away the tears and got to her feet. What she needed, she decided, was another cup of hot coffee.

Mandy called an hour later, full of enthusiasm. "Lovewear wants you at nine," she told Teddi. "Can you make it? It's for an interview on three commercials for their new line of jeans!"

"Can I make it? Are you kidding?" Teddi laughed. "I'll crawl there on my knees if I can't catch a cab. Thanks, Mandy!"

She snatched up her portfolio with the composites safely tucked away inside, and paused just long enough to grab her small shoulder bag before she rushed into the elevator, cursing the incredibly high heels that she couldn't take time to change.

She darted through the door and out onto the sidewalk, making a wild dash for the first cab she saw pulling up at the curb. She misjudged the step, and in an incredible series of stumbles, worsened by the high heels, she managed to land herself just past the cab's front bumper, right in the path of an oncoming car.

Wide-eyed, helpless, she could see the disaster coming, but there was nothing in the world she could do in that split second to save herself. Like a spectator watching her own body, she observed with an inhuman calmness. Then she felt a sudden cold emptiness, numbness, and screams followed her down into the darkness.

Chapter Nine

The next fe[...] a haze of terrible pain, urgent voices, [...] rens, followed by visions of white [...] and silvery metal and, finally, complete numbn[...]s.

When she regained full consciousness, she was aware of pain in her face and her right leg and a bruised feeling over most of her body. Added to it all, she had a splitting headache.

Her eyes opened slowly, staring up at a small, dark-eyed nurse who was taking her blood pressure. There was a thermometer in her mouth, and she watched the nurse take it out and read it.

"Hi," the nurse said gently. "Feel up to a few questions now?"

"I think...so." Teddi's hands went to her face, and she felt a thick padding of bandages from her temple to her chin.

"It's all right," the nurse said quickly. "Nothing that won't heal."

Teddi swallowed. "What else?" she asked, turning to notice for the first time the bandages on her right leg where the covers were disheveled.

"Dr. Forbes will tell you all about it," she was assured, "when he makes his rounds in about—" the nurse checked her watch "—thirty minutes. But for now, I'm going to send down someone from admissions and let them get their information, if you're sure you're up to it?"

"Yes, I'm ... I'm fine," she said without any conviction. Her face and leg were obviously damaged in some way, and she could only guess at the rest of her injuries. She felt bruised all over.

"Just ... one thing," she said before the nurse left. "I was on my way to an interview ... I never made it, but could someone call the Amanda Roman Talent Agency and tell them where I am? I'm a model."

"Sure," the nurse assured her with a gentle smile. "I'll do it myself. What is your name, by the way? Did you know, you weren't even carrying any identification on you?"

"Left my wallet at home again," Teddi groaned. "Well, no harm done. I'm Teddi Whitehall."

"I'll make the call right now," the nurse said, and she was gone.

Time dragged horribly until Dr. Forbes, a kind, white-haired gentleman, walked in to tell her what was wrong.

"Your leg was badly lacerated," he began quietly, seating himself on the edge of the bed. "We had to do some cosmetic surgery as we repaired the damage. That's why your thigh may feel a bit uncomfortable. That's where we took a patch of skin for the graft. Not to worry, it'll grow back quickly enough. The same can be done for your face when the stitches come out, if you think you want that. The scar will heal completely, in time, without it," he added, watching her face grow white.

"My...my leg?" she whispered.

He drew in a slow breath. "My dear, there's just no simple way to put it. We can repair flesh and bone, to a degree, and cosmetic surgery will put it nearly right again. But we can't make it as good as new, you understand. Those ligaments are going to take a long time to heal. You may be left with a slight limp. Of course, further surgery can be performed, if necessary."

"Of course," she murmured, barely hearing him.

"And you have a concussion," he added with a faint smile, "as you've probably suspected if your head is throbbing as much as I expect."

"It is uncomfortable," she agreed, touching it.

"I'll have the nurse give you something for it." He patted her hand. "Don't worry about it today. Give yourself time to adjust to the shock. I realize it must seem like the end of world to a beautiful woman such as yourself, and a model as well. But you know, in the long run, most changes are beneficial, regardless of the disasters they might seem at first. The difficulty is not in situations, my dear, but in our attitude toward them. Your scars will fade before you realize it. A few weeks from now, you'll be moving around quite well."

She nodded, her mind whirling with shock. What was she going to do? The hospital bill would be formidable, and it was clear that she'd be out of work for several weeks if not longer with these disfiguring marks. How could she cope?

"Bear in mind what I said," he told her, rising. "We'll keep you here another day or so, and then you'll have to be careful about getting around, not putting too much pressure on that leg. Once you're home, you'll do very well, I'm sure."

"Yes," she agreed. "Thank you."

When he was gone, she huddled under the bedcovers, staring at the blank television set and the empty bed in the semiprivate room. Teddi couldn't ever remember feeling so alone. She was hurt, deserted, with no one to care about her. They'd asked if she wanted them to notify anyone besides Mandy. But she'd said no. There was no one to tell. Dilly would only be irritated at the interruption. King didn't care, and he'd forbidden her to call Jenna. She burst into tears, burying her face in her hands. She'd always been strong, because she'd had to be. But for a moment, she gave in to grief. Everything seemed so hopeless.

The next morning, things looked no brighter, but Teddi was beginning to think she might cope better a little farther down the road. Toward that end, she asked about being released from the hospital. In the first place, she explained to Dr. Forbes, she just didn't have the funds to cover a long hospital stay and she had no insurance. In the second place, she'd feel much more comfortable in familiar surroundings.

"Well," he frowned thoughtfully, staring at her with his thin lips pursed, "is there someone there to look after you? You won't be able to do much walking, you know, and those dressings will need to be changed."

"Oh, my aunt will be there," she assured him, cringing mentally at the deliberate lie.

He considered the matter for a minute. "All right," he agreed finally. "But you'll need to come to my office in a week and have those stitches removed."

"I'll be there with bells on," she promised.

"Just call my office and make an appointment," he advised. "Now, look me straight in the eye and promise me you'll stay in bed for at least three more days before you try to get up and run road races."

She looked him in the eye and promised. It was a shame that she burst into a giggle on the last word.

It was hard-going alone in the apartment. She could barely hobble to the kitchen, even with the aid of a walking stick, and every step hurt like the devil. If it hadn't been for a friendly neighborhood grocery that delivered, she probably would have starved to death. Dilly hadn't left any food in the place, and the meager supplies Teddi had gotten in when she arrived had dwindled to a carton of spoiled milk and some stale bread.

Despite her diminished finances, Teddi gave the delivery boy a large tip after he was kind enough to not only put the groceries away for her, but fix her some soup and coffee as well.

"After all," she coaxed when he tried to give it back, "without you I'd have starved."

"Oh, I doubt that," he replied with a grin.

She finished her coffee after he'd left and leaned back against the sofa. As she thought of the assignments she was probably missing, tears misted her eyes. Her fingers went to the bandage on her cheek. She'd mustered enough courage that morning to change it, and had cried bitterly at the sight of the red antiseptic-smeared gashes with their ugly black stitches. She looked like an advertisement for a horror movie.

She was so wrapped up in her morose reflections that it was several moments before she realized the phone was ringing. She stretched over to pick up the receiver.

"Hello?"

"Teddi!" Jenna cried, relieved. "My gosh, I thought I'd never find you! I've been calling the apartment every morning for days looking for you. Where were you, what's going on?"

"I've been . . . working," Teddi murmured. "How are you?" she asked, fighting down tears at the sound of her friend's voice.

"I'd be fine if I were an only child," came the grumbling reply. "King's been just awful. Oh, Teddi, what did he say to you? Do you know he got stone-drunk the night you left and couldn't lift his head the next morning? He left suddenly for Australia that afternoon... but never mind that, your agency said something about an accident. I called there in desperation, you see..."

"I flung myself under a Cadillac," Teddi murmured, drying her tears on the hem of her blouse.

"You what?"

"I stumbled off the curb in my mad dash for a cab," Teddi said sheepishly. "I was rushing to an interview when I slipped and did a balletic routine—totally impromptu, you understand—under the wheels of a bright yellow Caddie. Didn't I have good taste?"

"Are you all right?" Jenna persisted. "Why were you in the hospital?"

"I mangled my leg and got a few cuts and bruises. Other than that, I'm my usual self."

"Are you there alone? Is Dilly home?"

"Heavens no, thank goodness," she replied with a sigh. "Gosh, it's good to hear your voice. I was getting maudlin, sitting here by myself."

"Are you sure it's only some cuts and bruises?" Jenna asked shrewdly, knowing from long acquaintance how her friend tended to minimize things.

"Only!" Teddi laughed. "It's my right leg, you know, the one I kick people with!"

"You know what I mean. And where are the cuts? And what did you mean about your leg being mangled?"

"Nothing much," Teddi lied. "I'll be fine in a few days."

"Come up here and stay with me. I'll look after you."

"No!" Teddi said quickly, visions of King appearing before her eyes.

"He's just come back from Australia," Jenna said, reading the other girl's mind. "Subdued, quiet, hardly the same man who left here the day after you did. The men are shaking in their boots, waiting for the explosion. Whatever he did or said, Teddi, it's hurt him, too."

"You're sweet to offer," Teddi said, "but I can't possibly leave right now. I've got to be here if my agency calls. I could still model hands, you know, or lips."

"Oh," murmured her blissfully ignorant friend. "Are you telling me the truth?"

"Truly I am. Look, how are you and Blakely getting along?"

"Blakely has decided that I am worth fighting King for," she informed Teddi smugly. "He has told King that he is marrying me in December, whether King likes it or not, and if he can't work on Gray Stag, there are lots of other properties around the area that will hire him. How about that?"

"I'm so happy for you," she said genuinely. "Can I come to the wedding?"

"Silly, you're going to be maid of honor. So do hurry up and heal, won't you?"

"With all possible speed," Teddi promised.

Hours later, reflecting on that conversation while she curled up on the sofa in her fluffy blue bathrobe with her aching leg propped on the cushions, she wondered if Jenna had swallowed the explanation. Her friend tended to be suspicious even at the best of times.

Well, she thought miserably, at least Jenna's call had brightened her day a little. She wondered why King had darted off to Australia—of course, he was a busy man, and the ranch was his life. Ranches, she corrected herself. Her eyes closed. How was she going to avoid him at Jenna's wedding? That was thinking a long way ahead, of course, and she'd had years of practice at dodging him. She'd think of something. No matter how much it hurt, she was going to have to find some way of never seeing him again. It would make the long years ahead a little more bearable, without the sight of him to taunt her with things that might have been.

The doorbell clanged loudly and she put down the magazine she was leafing through and hobbled to the door with the help of the walking stick. She'd ordered some more groceries from the store. It was probably the nice delivery boy back again.

She opened the door and stared wide-eyed at the tall, gray-suited man scowling down at her.

"Hello, Teddi," Kingston Devereaux said quietly.

She felt herself freezing, and all the hurtful things he'd said and done came back in a rush. She stared up at him with darkening eyes.

"I...I'm not dressed for visitors," she said. "Thank you for stopping by, but..."

He eased past her, closed the door, and scooped her up in his hard arms. The walking stick fell from her fingers as he carried her back to the sofa, and she succumbed for an instant to the need to be held, touched by him.

"Only a scratch, is that how the song goes?" he growled, staring at the bandage on her cheek and the one on her leg, the scratches and bruises visible where the sleeves of her silky green gown fell away from her forearms.

"Will you put me down?" she asked, struggling.

He eased her down onto the sofa and let her go with obvious reluctance, seating himself close beside her.

"How bad is it?" he asked, indicating the bandage on her leg.

She shrugged. "I'll heal."

"How bad is it?" he repeated curtly.

"Some torn ligaments and a nasty scar," she grumbled. Her hand went to the bandage, and her lips trembled betrayingly as her eyes fell. "The stitches come out next week."

"What else?" he persisted, his eyes dark and stormy.

"Concussion. Some bruises."

He drew in a deep, slow breath. "Why the hell didn't you call me?"

Her eyebrows arched, her eyes widened. "Wouldn't that be a bit like having a scratched chicken call the fox for first aid?" she burst out.

"I suppose it must seem that way, after what I did to you," he agreed gently. His eyes searched hers, as if he were inspecting a beloved painting he hadn't seen in years. "But I would have come, all the same."

"From Australia?" she asked.

"From hell," he replied, "if I'd been there. And it felt as if I were, if you want to know. I haven't slept a full night since you left, remembering the way you looked.... Teddi, for the love of heaven, why didn't you tell me years ago?"

"How would I have gone about it?" she hedged, looking down at the tiny buttons on her satin gown. "We were worlds apart all those years, and you wouldn't have cared anyway." She laughed. "You'd probably have accused me of leading the man on in the first place—"

"Stop it," he ground out, running an irritated hand through his thick hair. "Don't you think I feel enough like a heel, as it is?"

He was the picture of a man tormented by regret eating him alive, and Teddi's compassionate heart was touched. But she didn't want his guilt. She only wanted his love, and that was out of her reach forever.

"It's all right," she said quietly, toying with a button on the flared skirt of the gown.

"Have you been here all alone, since the accident?" he asked.

She nodded. A tiny smile touched her mouth. "The delivery boy brought me a few groceries and made me some soup."

She heard his harsh intake of breath and looked up to see torment in his gray eyes.

"You're coming home with me," he said. "If I have to carry you out of here kicking and screaming, I'm taking you where you'll be properly cared for."

"You've made a habit of that lately," she said coldly.

He nodded. "I'll concede that point, I've been unjustifiably cruel to you." He stuck his hands in his pockets, stretching the material of his trousers across his flat belly, his powerful thighs. "I had a totally distorted picture of you from the beginning. I cultivated it," he added with a strange half smile. "It was my last line of defense. When I finally admitted the truth about you to myself, all the walls went down." He glanced at her. "I haven't taken more than a drink or two in years, but the day you left I took Joey into Calgary with me, and we came home at three in the morning singing 'Waltzing Matilda' at the top of our lungs. Mother was shocked. The next day I took off for the Australian property in a daze, and I feel as if I've stayed in it ever since. Teddi, I know there was nothing between you and Billingsly."

She stared quietly into his eyes. "Did Bruce call you?" she asked.

He shook his head. "He didn't have to. Jenna told me everything. Not that it would have mattered, once I came to my senses. You couldn't have been the way you were with me in the woods that day if there'd been another man. And no money-hungry woman works the way you work to earn your keep."

It was nice to be believed at last, but was it guilt making him say these things?

"It ... it was kind of you to come all this way to tell me," she murmured, confused.

"I came for more than that," he said. "I want to touch you. Are you going to let me, and not back away this time?"

Her breath almost stopped as she looked into those soft, quiet gray eyes, the face that she'd loved for an eternity.

"Not out of guilt, King," she pleaded unsteadily.

"Not out of guilt, darling," he said, his voice deepening with emotion. His fingers brushed her neck, her chin, the soft hollow in her throat.

"Your heart's trying to climb out," he murmured, watching the wild pulsing under his fingers. His eyes dropped to the silk over her taut breasts and he stared at it with a burning gaze. As if he couldn't help himself, his fingers began to trail down to that tautness, his knuckles brushing over her gently.

"No." She caught her breath, gripping his hair-covered wrist with cold, nervous fingers.

"I've lain awake nights remembering," he ground out, holding her eyes. "The way you felt, the way you looked.... I don't imagine it's going to be easy, but from now on, I'm going to handle you like priceless porcelain."

Her heart began to throb wildly at the light in his eyes, the deepening tone of his voice. Watch it, girl, she told herself, he's a master at teasing women.

"You aren't going to handle me at all," she said with a wobble in her voice.

"You're going to want me," he whispered, leaning over her with his big hands on either side of her head. "You already do, but you've put all the old walls back up because of what I did to you. I'm going to knock them down, Miss Whitehall," he promised softly. "One by one, day by day, until you're as hungry for me as I am for you."

Her cheeks flushed. "Never," she breathed. "I don't . . . I don't want that with you."

"Darling," he murmured, bending, "of course you do."

His mouth brushed against hers teasingly, tracing the outline of her full, soft lips, lightly pressing, nudging, until they parted helplessly. She felt his own lips parting and tasted smoke and coffee and mint as she gave in to the long hunger for him, the loneliness and heartache and sleepless nights when she would have given anything to touch him.

Her fingers went hesitantly to his shirt, and he caught them, lifting them to his face, moving them caressingly against his cheek.

"Yes," he whispered huskily, "like that. Soft little fingers, I could feel them when I closed my eyes, tracing patterns across my face . . . on my body."

She caught her breath as his mouth eased between her lips intimately.

"You've never touched me," he whispered tormentingly. "Don't you want to feel my skin, to touch it the way I've touched yours?"

She moaned, hating what he could do to her with words, hating the images that were flashing through her mind.

"Come here, darling," he whispered, lifting her gently against him to lie across his legs while his mouth took more and more from hers. Her fingers dug into his shoulders through the expensive fabric of his jacket, her mouth trying to match the expertness of his, trying to give what he was demanding. What she lacked in experience, she made up for with pure love, but that was something he'd never know, because she'd never have the courage to tell him. He'd think it was desire, like what he was feeling for her, a purely physical thing.

"I love the way you feel in satin," he murmured gruffly, letting his hands mold the soft curves of her body.

"You shouldn't ... touch me that way," she managed.

"Nothing we do together is wrong, if we both want it," he said, lifting his disheveled blond head to look down at her. "Teddi, would you ever let another man touch you like this?" he asked solemnly.

She looked frankly horrified, and he nodded, his eyes watchful. "And I know that," he continued. "I'm not going to hold you in contempt for wanting my hands on this sweet young body, for letting me see it. I don't play bedroom games with virgins, surely to God you know that by now?''

Her eyes widened curiously. ''What do you want, then?'' she whispered.

He drew in a steadying breath. ''Honey, you're not that naive, surely?''

''You . . . want me?'' she asked shyly.

''Desperately,'' he replied quietly.

''But—''

He touched her mouth with a silencing finger. ''I'm not going to seduce you. I could, very easily. But that's not what I want. I'm going to teach you how to trust me again. Then,'' he murmured, bending to kiss her very gently, ''I'm going to teach you how to make love.''

''I won't have an affair with you,'' she told him.

He smiled. ''Won't you?''

''King . . .''

''Not now.'' He smoothed the hair away from her cheeks, sketching the soft lines of her face with eyes that blazed with curbed hunger. ''Still nervous of me?''

''A little.'' She looked up at him, feeling as if all her dreams had suddenly come true. It couldn't be real; he must be the product of her insane longing for him. She reached up hesitantly to touch his hard face. ''You're stronger than I am, and I know now how it is when you . . . when you want a woman.''

''No, you don't,'' he replied, holding her hand against his cheek. ''I was half out of my mind with jealousy. That wasn't lovemaking, it was pure revenge. Don't confuse the two." He searched her eyes slowly. "Teddi, men can be animals, but I could never be one with you past a certain point. Even that day in the den, when I looked at you, I could feel myself melting inside. Another minute, and you would have had no reason to be afraid of me. Not one." He touched her hot cheek and smiled faintly. "Despite what I did, I'm a gentle lover, darling. I'd be endlessly patient with you."

The flush got worse, but she didn't drop her eyes, she couldn't seem to look away. She was aware of the warmth and scent of him, the strength in his arms, the softness in his eyes as he looked back at her.

"You'd have to teach me...how to please you," she heard herself say.

"You already please me," he said, his fingers moving gently on her softness, the sound of them stroking the satin like the whisper of the wind. "Where are you bruised?" he breathed, looking down. "Here?" he asked, letting his hand linger over her heart as he caught her gaze.

"A...little," she whispered.

As she watched, he bent his head and she felt the hot press of his lips even through the fabric, in a caress she'd never shared with a man.

She moaned, catching his head with hands that didn't seem to know whether to push or pull.

Before the pleasure fully registered on her, he sat up, pulling her with him. "Someday," he breathed huskily, "I'm going to do that when there's no material in my way."

Just the thought of it made her heart run away, her breath catch in her throat.

She looked at him, her fingers on the buttons of the gown, and her gaze was full of hunger for his eyes, his lips.

He caught the expression in her eyes and drew in a sharp breath. "Don't," he cautioned, getting to his feet. "I want you too much already."

She stared, puzzled, her hands stilled as she tried to understand what he wanted.

"Teddi, I haven't felt like this since I was sixteen years old," he ground out, ramming his hands into his pockets as he turned away from her. "And that being the case, I think you'd better go and put on something that's a little more concealing. The whole world may have gone permissive, but I have a few things in common with my Victorian ancestors, and I don't want to take you into my bed on an impulse."

"I don't understand what you want," she murmured, rising.

"You will." He turned, moving close to brush a tender kiss across her forehead. "Now go and dress and throw something into a bag. I didn't come all this way to be turned down."

"Did anyone ever tell you that you have a Julius Caesar complex?" she asked, holding out her hand for the walking stick he'd picked up from the floor.

"Only where you're concerned, darling," he drawled with a wicked smile. "I do admit, in that respect, to an infatuation with the idea of conquest."

She hurried away before he could see the redness in her cheeks.

Teddi couldn't remember ever being so much a part of a family. Miss Peake, thin and tart and motherly, hovered like a good fairy, trying to tempt Teddi's appetite with soups and delicate little pastries.

"But I'm perfectly able to get up," Teddi had protested the day King brought her home.

Miss Peake had looked down her hatchet nose with a sniff. "After a concussion?" she asked haughtily. "With that leg? Bruised from head to toe? You get out of that bed, Miss Teddi, and I'll carry you back in here myself!"

And that had been the end of it. Teddi had no doubt at all that Miss Peake was capable of making good on her threat. Mary and Jenna had laughed at the confrontation, but not in front of their formidable housekeeper.

"I can see her now," Jenna whispered merrily, "hauling you over her shoulder..."

"She wouldn't have to," Mary laughed. "King would beat her to it. No, my dear," she told the invalid with a kindly pat on the hand, "you stay where you are until King and Miss Peake feel that you're able to wander about again."

She left, and Jenna stared after her with both eyebrows raised. "Poor Mama." She shook her head. "She hasn't been able to change the furniture or make a major decision since King and Miss Peake took over the property."

Teddi laughed in spite of herself. "You make them sound like an invading army."

Jenna smiled. "What a delightful analogy!"

"They do tend to stick together," Teddi said, grinning.

"Did I tell you what King said to Blakely, when Blakely told him we were getting married and to do his worst?" Jenna asked.

Teddi shook her head.

"He congratulated him. Not a word about anything. He even offered to give us a tract in the Valley!"

"That was nice." Teddi smiled.

"Nice? It was incredible! Blakely couldn't believe his ears." Jenna stretched lazily. "Well, I'd better get out of here and let you rest. If you need anything, yell, okay?"

"Okay. Thanks, Jenna. You're all so kind…" Teddi faltered, trying to find words.

"You're family," Jenna said simply. She smiled. "See you later."

King looked in on her from time to time, friendly, caring, and Teddi couldn't help wondering if she was in the right house. He seemed altogether different now, and despite her wariness of him, she began to warm to his new attitude. She could relax, listen to his plans for Gray Stag, to his sometimes amusing revelations about what was going on around the ranch while she convalesced. But he didn't touch her. Not at all, not once. It was as if he was intent on building friendship between them before he attempted to move any closer physically.

Among them, the family managed to keep her mind off her future. But she still found time to brood. And one day King caught her at it.

"First get well," he chided when he came in unexpectedly, and his gray eyes danced under the familiar wide-brimmed hat. "Then brood. One day at a time, darling, that's how it's done."

"Change places with me and try that," Teddi challenged.

He shook his head, smiling wickedly. "I won't change places, but I might be tempted to join you."

She averted her eyes. Ridiculous how he could make her pulse jump with mere words. "It's a twin bed."

"All the better," he murmured dryly.

She glared at him. "I told you I didn't want an affair with you."

"So you keep saying," he sighed. "I'll just have to pay more attention to changing your mind."

"No fair," she muttered.

He only laughed. "Everything's fair now," he corrected. "What would you like for a snack?" he asked, moving closer. He was wearing denim jeans and a shirt with dusty boots, and he looked like a working man. "How about some strawberries?"

Her big eyes lit up. "Strawberries?"

"I'm having Miss Peake bring them in a few minutes, along with some whipped cream."

"A week ago, I'd have refused the whipped cream," she sighed. "But now, I don't suppose a few extra pounds will matter."

"My thoughts exactly." He stared down at her thin body under the sheets with concern. "You're practically all bones now."

He sat down beside her, his hard, warm thigh touching her side. He leaned forward to brush her hair away from her cheek. He'd already taken off the bandage, and he put the medicine on her cheek and on her leg, every night himself, trusting it to no one else.

Her eyes went to his chiseled mouth and she stared at it with an intensity she wasn't even aware of. She couldn't help herself. It had been so long since he'd kissed her, held her. She wanted him to...

"Do you want to kiss me?" he murmured softly. He leaned down, within touching distance, holding her stunned eyes. "Come on, Teddi. Don't hold back."

Her lower lip trembled. "I won't beg..."

"Oh, the devil with begging," he growled, parting her lips expertly with his. "What does it matter who starts it if we both want it?" His breath sighed into her mouth, his teeth nibbled at it tenderly while his hands tangled slowly in her hair. His heart pounded heavily over her breasts as he eased down against them.

"King..." Her hands moved up, dislodging his hat to smooth the silky hair at his temples. Her eyes closed, her body lifted, grinding up against his. It was heaven. Heaven!

"Touch me," he whispered, teasing her mouth with kisses that burned like fire.

"I am," she whispered, nibbling back at his mouth, eagerly learning all the sweet lessons he was teaching her.

"Not the way I want you to," he murmured. He found one of her hands and pressed it against the damp front of his denim shirt, where his heart was shuddering in his chest. "Men are like cats, darling, they like to be stroked, didn't you know?" he murmured.

Her hands smoothed the fabric in slow, hard strokes while he kissed her.

"Teddi," he groaned. He held himself poised over her, his fingers going impatiently to the buttons of his shirt, tearing them open. "Now," he growled, thrusting one of her hands inside it, onto the warm, damp skin of his chest. "Like that."

She stared up at him, feeling a new kind of hunger, aware of exquisite sensations as her fingers tangled in the thick, crisp hair. He looked sensuously male like this, his body half-bare, his hair ruffled, his mouth slightly swollen, his eyes narrow with undisguised ardor.

"Macho," she breathed, looking straight into his eyes. "Much, much man . . ."

His hands tightened on her sleek, dark head. "You're not bad yourself, kid," he whispered with faint humor. "Harder," he added, watching her hands with a half smile. "Touch, don't tickle."

"I'm trying," she murmured, "but I'm having to fight my way through the underbrush . . ."

"You little vixen," he accused. His mouth crushed down over hers, parting her lips almost savagely as he took what he needed from her. She felt the velvety hardness of his tongue easing into the sweet softness of her mouth, invading, taking, and a surge of wild feeling welled up in her. Her long nails dug into his chest before she lifted her arms to cling to him, raising her body against his warm hands, hands that knew where to touch, how to touch, to hold. A wild little moan whispered from her mouth into his, shocking him.

He drew back a breath, watching her. "Too hard?" he whispered, his hands gentle where they rested over the soft upthrust of her body.

"Oh, no," she whispered back, trembling under his expert caresses.

His thumbs stroked tenderly and she gasped. "You fit my hands so perfectly...woman, you feel like silk and satin, and you make my head spin when I touch you like this. You're not afraid of me anymore, are you?"

She shook her head slowly, watching him with her heart in her eyes.

His hands moved again, and she arched helplessly, dazed at the newness of what he was teaching her. "All woman," he breathed. "Soft and wild and giving. This is what a woman should feel when her man touches her. Oh, yes, darling," he whispered, bending slowly. "Yes, just like that, come up toward me. Darling, darling, move just...like...that...." His mouth caught hers again, and with a sunburst of sensation she felt his fingers opening her gown to the waist, gentle hands, so gentle, touching her in new ways, tenderly awakening sensations she had never known until now.

Slowly, the whole warm weight of his big body eased onto hers. She felt every sinew of him, every male contour; she felt his breathing as if it were her own. She seemed to have become a part of him.

Her body melted into his, softness giving way to hair-matted hardness, her body bare to the waist as his was, her flesh under his. She clung, unafraid, loving him until it was like torture to be so close and yet still not close enough.

Trembling, she drew her lips just a whisper away from his, shifting sensuously under him as she sought to get even closer, and he groaned.

"Please," she whispered achingly. "Please help me."

He held her face gently in hands that trembled, his face tense, his body strung as taut as a rope as he stared down at her with tormented eyes.

"I can't," he whispered, easing his weight from her. He settled alongside her trembling body, and gently drew her close, his hands soothing now, easing the ache from her body.

"King," she whispered against his warm throat. "King."

"Next time," he said at her ear, "we won't stop. I'll finish it."

"I couldn't have said no," she moaned.

He laughed softly, tenderly. "I wonder what Miss Peake would have said if she walked in and I had given way to my instincts?"

"Miss Peake?" she echoed, dazed.

"You do remember I asked her to bring you some berries and cream?" he asked.

She gasped, drawing back to look at him. "I forgot!"

He cocked an eyebrow, letting his eyes drop to her open gown. She caught the edges together, flushing as her eyes met his.

"Don't be shy with me," he chided. "You're lovely."

"You make me feel that way," she corrected, looking at him quietly. "King . . . why?"

"Why what?" he murmured, throwing his long legs over the side of the bed. He sat up and lit a cigarette while she fumbled with her buttons.

"What do you want from me?" she persisted.

"Everything," he replied quietly, towering over her with his shirt still unbuttoned.

She searched his eyes, confused. "For how long?"

He shrugged. "Who knows?"

"And how about what I want?" she replied softly. He wasn't offering commitment. He was agreeing to nothing more than a few nights together, with no strings on either side.

"I know what you want, darling," he murmured wickedly. "You want me."

"And is desire enough to satisfy you?" she challenged.

He gave her a strange, intent look. "I suppose it will have to be."

At that moment, Miss Peake came in, carrying a tray with iced tea and a bowl of fresh strawberries and cream.

"King picked these for you," Miss Peake told her with a quick, appraising glance at King's open shirt. "Thought you might like some whipped cream on them, too."

King ignored the disapproving glance and moved toward the door. "I've got work to do," he said without looking back at Teddi.

"Too bad the cattle won't herd themselves," Miss Peake remarked.

King turned, glancing quietly at Teddi. "Isn't it?" he murmured.

She glanced up at him. "Thanks for the therapy," she murmured wickedly.

He cocked an eyebrow. "Is that what it felt like?" he asked. "I'll have to work on my technique." And he turned and went out the door, leaving her puzzled and breathless.

For the next few days, King reverted to being polite, friendly, and nothing more. It was as if he were giving her breathing space, time to consider the final step, to decide if she could settle for the only relationship he was willing to offer.

She agonized over it. Loving him as she did, she didn't know if she could ever accept an affair. It would be even harder to let go afterward than it was now. Because she would have had the joy of belonging to him. And that would bind her to him in new ways, with strings that were impossible to break.

He'd practically admitted that desire was all he felt for her, when he'd said that desire would be enough to satisfy him. But would it be enough for her? The physical relationship would be wonderful, of course, but was it enough? She loved just sitting with him in the living room, watching TV. She loved watching him over the dinner table, riding beside him and talking on lazy summer mornings. She enjoyed him in ways that had nothing to do with desire. The newness of physical possession would soon wear off, and what would they have left? Teddi would feel like a cast-off shoe, and she didn't think she could bear it.

She made up her mind slowly, but irrevocably. And when she felt well enough to pick up her life, and the stitches had been removed by a local doctor, she decided to go back to New York. The scar, while still noticeable on her cheek, could be covered with cosmetics, and she could walk well enough to work. She would work, she told herself, because she had to. And perhaps her career would take the place of a brief affair with King. Perhaps it would at least help fill the empty space.

Tearing off a hand would have hurt less, but she knew she had to tell King what she was going to do.

She followed him out the door after breakfast, she had made up her mind. She closed the door behind them, leaving the family at the breakfast table.

"What is it?" he asked gently. "Something important?"

"Yes." She licked her dry lips, fascinated by the way his eyes followed the movement so intently. He looked sensuously masculine this morning, in his tight-fitting jeans and brown-patterned shirt, the wide-brimmed hat cocked over one brow, his face faintly smiling as he looked at her.

"Well?" he prodded.

It was all she could do to keep from throwing her body against his and begging him to carry her off someplace. She shook her head to dispel that notion.

"I'm going home tomorrow."

He looked as if somebody had hit him on the head with a length of steel pipe.

"What?"

"I said, I'm going home tomorrow," she repeated. "I need to get back to work, and the scars are fading fast, thank goodness. I can cover them with cosmetics..."

"You're leaving me?" he burst out. "Just like that!"

She faltered, shocked at the fury in his hard face.

"I..." she began.

"Is it that Lothario accountant after all?" he growled. "Or is it just that you can't force yourself to make a commitment?"

"Look who's talking about commitments!" she threw back. "Old Footloose and Fancy-Free!"

"What did you expect, a ninety-nine-year contract, for God's sake?" he growled.

"No, thanks," she returned, "I couldn't take ninety-nine years of you!"

"Scared?" he chided.

"Not of you," she retorted. "I just want more than you've got to offer, that's all."

"Like what?" he challenged, his eyes blazing. "Flashy fashion shows and leering men?"

"It's my career!" she cried.

His face froze over. "Then, if that's what you want, go back to it," he said with ice in his voice. "Go today. I'll have someone drive you to the airport this afternoon, in fact."

She gasped. "What?"

There were storms brewing in his cold gray eyes, and a livid fury that she didn't understand. "You heard me," he ground out. "Get packed!" He turned on his heel and stomped down the steps.

Tears poured down her cheeks as his words sank in. He was throwing her off the property! She could barely believe her own ears. Did he hate her so much that he couldn't bear the sight of her anymore? Or was it just his masculine pride, damaged because she wasn't the pushover he'd expected her to be?

She went wobbling up the stairs to her room in a daze and started packing, wondering how she was going to explain this to Jenna and Mary.

She grimaced. Well, she'd just let King explain it. He could tell them whatever he liked. She'd make up some story about an assignment or something, and let him take it from there. Arrogant beast!

It only took a few minutes to get her things together. King thought she preferred modeling to him, and perhaps it was better that way. She didn't want him to find out how desperately she was in love with him. Her pride would be crushed if he knew.

She closed the bag and picked it up, taking one last look around the bedroom to make sure she hadn't forgotten anything. She turned, closing the door quietly behind her. Above all, she must act as if nothing were wrong, she mustn't let him know how devastated she really was.

She walked down the staircase, to find King in deep conversation with Jenna at the front door. He looked up when he saw Teddi in her white linen pantsuit and the same pale blue wrap blouse she'd worn the day he took her to Banff.

Something flashed in his gray eyes at the sight of that blouse, but his face gave nothing away.

"I was just telling Jenna about your new assignment," he told Teddi curtly, daring her to deny it.

She cleared her throat and tried to look radiant, wary of Jenna's sharp eyes on her as she went the rest of the way down the staircase.

"Yes, I'm so excited I can hardly stand it," she told her best friend with a forced smile. "Imagine, two commercials . . . !"

King looked uncomfortable and Jenna narrowed her eyes. "I thought it was a trunk show in Miami," she said.

Teddi shifted the small suitcase from one hand to the other. "Uh, yes, that's what it is . . . a trunk show and two commercials in Miami," she murmured, her voice fading away.

"What," Jenna asked, looking from one to the other, "is going on?"

King took Teddi's arm. "We'd better go or you'll miss your flight," he said gruffly, drawing her out the door. "Jenna, I'll be back in a couple of hours," he told his sister, and slammed the door before she could ask any more questions.

"You might have given me time to say good-bye to Jenna and your mother," Teddi said angrily as he put her in the passenger seat of the Ferrari.

"You can wave at them, can't you?" he asked tautly. He got in and started the engine with an angry motion, barely giving her time to wave at the two stunned women standing on the front steps before he roared away toward Calgary.

She glanced at his set profile. He hadn't even bothered to change out of his work clothes. His boots were dusty and his hat looked as if it had seen better days. But of course nobody paid any attention to clothing in a busy airport. Her eyes unconsciously worshipped him. It was only just dawning on her that by saying "no" she was banishing herself from him forever. She'd never see him again after today.

Tears formed in her big brown eyes and she turned her face away before he could see them. She'd been lonely before, and she'd survived. But having tasted his ardor, it was going to be worse now. The thought of the lonely years ahead hurt terribly.

She brushed at a tear inconspicuously and straightened in her seat. This would never do. She'd have to get hold of herself.

As if sensing her uneasiness, he turned on the radio. A constant stream of music and news filled the silence between them as his powerful Ferrari ate up the miles. He was pushing it even harder than usual, as if he couldn't wait to be rid of her.

He pulled up in the parking lot at the busy international airport a few minutes later and cut off the engine. But he didn't make a move to get out of the car. His big hands gripped the steering wheel hard for an instant, then he sat back in his seat and lit a cigarette.

"Did you have to wear that particular blouse?" he asked in a cold voice.

She avoided his piercing gaze. "It was the only clean one I had," she said quietly. "I was going to wash the others this afternoon."

"You'll have to buy a ticket," he said. "I didn't stop to make reservations for you." He studied her with stormy eyes. "Do you have the fare?"

She swallowed. "Of course," she lied. She had planned to borrow money from Jenna.

He took a sharp draw from the cigarette. "Of course," he laughed shortly, reading her like a book. "I'll put it on my charge card. You can pay me back when you start working again."

She couldn't refuse. All she had in her purse was a hundred dollars. She'd spent every other penny on the hospital bill and food. But having to accept charity from him was the final indignity. A single tear made a path down her cheek, but she turned away before he saw it.

"Thank you," she said, composing herself.

He took another quick, jerky draw from the cigarette. "Will you be able to work?"

"I think so," she said proudly. "I'll have to, if I
want to enroll for the next semester. I should be able
to do trunk shows at least, the scars don't show at a
distance. And I can cover them now with cosmetics.
I'll be fine. Just fine."

He made an impatient sound and turned to stare out
the window. His hat seemed to bother him. He ripped
it off and tossed it onto the back seat, running a hand
through his thick blond hair.

"It was your idea," he said accusingly, glaring
across the seat at her with fierce gray eyes.

She blinked. "What was?"

"Going back to New York," he growled. "Back to
your fabulous career, isn't that how the song goes?"

She bit her lower lip. It would only take a word, just
one word, to get his arms around her. But she couldn't
say it. She couldn't give in now, she couldn't sacrifice
her pride, her self-respect, for just a few nights with
him. . . .

She stared out the window, hating the departing
jets, hating the very sound of the engines as the huge
planes swept up to touch the clouds. One of those
would take her out of King's life forever.

As she brooded, she felt his fingers lightly touch her
hair. She turned, aching, and looked up into his eyes.

Time seemed to stretch like a violin string between
them while they searched each other's faces.

"Come here and kiss me good-bye," he growled
huskily and reached out to draw her against him.

With something between a sob and a moan, she let herself be tugged over the console and into his big arms. He leaned across to put out his cigarette before he gathered her close and bent to touch her mouth with his.

Breathing unevenly, she parted her lips, giving him back the kiss as gently as he gave it, tracing his hard face with fingers that trembled and went cold as they eased over his skin, into the thick, cool strands of hair at his temples.

"Don't nibble me," he whispered huskily. "Kiss me properly."

"I can't," she moaned, hiding her face in his warm throat. "I can't. Oh, King!" His name was a cry of anguish, and he reacted to it in an unexpected way.

His arms contracted, lifting her higher against his taut body. "Teddi, do you want to go?" he asked intently.

"I have to," she said simply, her voice muffled against his collar.

"Why?"

"You know why," she whispered, closing her eyes. It was heaven to be held like this, crushed against his big body, feeling his breath, his heartbeat, as if they were her own.

"I thought I did," he agreed. "But you aren't any more anxious to get out of this car than I am to let you. It isn't the philandering accountant, it never was. It isn't your damned career, either." He lifted her face and searched her eyes quietly. "I think you'd better tell me the truth, little one," he said softly, "before you destroy both our lives."

Her heart jerked in her chest. "Both?" she whispered incredulously, aware of a new note in his deep voice, a new light in his eyes.

A sob broke from her lips. "Oh, King, I don't want an affair," she wailed brokenly.

"Neither do I," he said quietly. His big hands smoothed the blouse away from her collarbone, easing under the fabric to almost, but not quite, touch her high, firm breasts. When she tried to pull away, he brought her gently back. "Don't fight me, darling," he said softly. "There's no need for it anymore. I'm only touching what belongs to me. You do. You always did."

Her eyes closed and she moaned. She was going to give in, she knew it, and she was going to hate both of them. Tears welled in her eyes. "I should go home," she breathed.

"Home is where I am," he said. His eyes searched hers. "I told you that once, and you thought I was kidding. I wasn't."

"King . . . ?" she whispered, aching for more than the light, teasing play of his fingers on her skin.

"I took one look at you when you were fifteen years old," he said in a voice too tender to be King's, "and hated you on sight because you were years too young for what I needed from you. By the time you were seventeen, I was in torment. That night during the storm, when I walked in to check on you—I found you lying there in that transparent gown, and I wanted you so much that I ached like a boy. But I had to walk out and leave you, because you were a virgin and I was afraid of what I might do." His eyes searched hers. "I wanted you to the point of madness that night, and it's only been a little less consuming since." As he spoke, his hands eased down under the loose blouse and gently took the weight of her soft, bare breasts, and she cried out with the sudden stab of pleasure.

"It's all right," he breathed, bending to kiss her trembling mouth. "I feel the same way when you touch me. Waves of blinding pleasure, washing over my body like fire..."

She lifted her arms around his neck, yielding her body completely to his slow, tormenting hands, trembling at the newness of allowing him to touch her, caress her this way. Her eyes looked straight into his, her teeth catching her lower lip to stifle the moans that welled up behind them.

"I had to let you think I hated you," he whispered gruffly, watching her. "It was the only protection I could give you. If I'd touched you like this even once, there would have been no stopping me. I was obsessed with you. It was agony to have you at the ranch, because I spent all those long days and nights forcing myself not to look at you, not to come too close." He expelled a harsh breath, and she read the torment in his eyes with a sense of wonder at what he seemed to be saying. "Then, at Easter, you started playing up to me, and I all but left the country. I taunted you, but I had to, can you understand that? I had to run you off before we got in over our heads, until I could get a grip on myself. And Billingsly had been filling my head full of lies...I was so jealous of you that I could have killed him!''

She searched his darkening eyes. She had to know— she had to know!

''King, do you care?'' she whispered shyly.

''Care?'' His eyes closed and opened again, gray flames rising in them. His hands moved to her face, cupping it, caressing it, and they began to tremble. ''I love you,'' he breathed. ''I love you so much that I feel as if I'm starving to death for you. I want to have you all my life. To share with. To laugh and cry with. To love with. You're my whole world, little one, didn't you know?''

Tears poured from her eyes like rain on the desert. She couldn't stop. Trembling fingers traced his face, her eyes openly adoring him, loving him.

He caught his breath at the emotion in her face, and his own eyes closed for an instant. ''My God, I've been blind, haven't I?'' he asked huskily. ''You're in love with me, aren't you?''

She nodded, her lower lip trembling, her eyes washed with tears as she tried to smile. ''I can't re- member when I didn't love you,'' she admitted bro- kenly. ''But I thought you just wanted an affair...''

''I do,'' he teased gently, his eyes devouring her. ''Sixty years' worth, and a few sons and daughters to love, and you in my bed every night, even the nights when we're too tired to make love.'' His eyes burned with emotion as they searched hers. ''I want you in ways that go far beyond anything strictly physical, although," he added, easing the blouse off one shoulder to smooth his lips along her silken flesh, "I could make a meal of you right now."

She nuzzled her face into his throat with a joyful sigh. "I love you," she whispered, "and I want you. But, darling, all our children will be illegitimate."

He laughed softly. "Then perhaps you'd better marry me before we discuss how many we're going to have."

"Did you say marry?" she asked, drawing back, confident enough to tease, seeing everything she would ever want or need in his worshipping eyes. "Old Footloose and Fancy-Free Devereaux actually proposing?"

"Do I recall your saying that you couldn't take ninety-nine years of me?" he countered.

"Was that before or after you threw me out of the house?" she retorted.

"I couldn't help myself," he confessed. "Having you around would have done me in, if you hadn't cared. I thought you were telling me that I mattered less than your career, that you couldn't see a future with me. I was devastated."

"You're my career," she said very quietly. "You and the children I'm going to give you. That's all I've ever wanted."

He seemed to have a hard time getting his breath. His eyes narrowed. "And college?"

"There's a college in Calgary," she reminded him. "And I've got all the time in the world to finish school now."

He leaned down and kissed her softly. "In that case, you'd better go ahead and enroll, hadn't you, before we're married. Then maybe you'll have time to finish. Although, I don't know what their policy is toward pregnant students...."

Her eyes held his. "That soon?" she whispered.

He drew her back down, easing her head into the crook of his arm. "Very soon," he breathed, as his mouth opened and parted the soft line of her lips. "Will you mind?"

Her only response was a soft cry that was lost in the hunger of his kiss, and for a long time the only sounds were of heightened breathing, wild, sharp moans and cries. When he finally let her draw a breath, her cheeks were flushed and her eyes were bright with excitement.

"We'd better go home before we get arrested," he said unsteadily. "You see what you do to me? I touch you and lose what little mind I have left."

She touched his mouth with soft, loving fingers. "It's always been that way for me."

He pressed her fingers to his lips and let them go reluctantly. "We're going to have a lot of explaining to do when we get back, I'm afraid," he sighed as he let her ease back into her own seat.

She laughed. "I won't mind. Will you?"

He shook his head. "Fancy a double wedding, do you?" he asked with a cocked eyebrow.

Her face brightened. "Oh, King, could we?"

He caught her hand as he started the car and put it in gear. ''We'll talk to Jenna and Blakely about it. Let's go home, darling.''

She clung to his hand as they left the airport, her eyes full of dreams. In the distance, the Rockies were welcoming, and the sun shone down in a clear blue sky. Teddi smiled up at her fiance with a warm, possessive gaze. He was right. Home was where he was. She leaned her head on his shoulder and closed her eyes.

*   *   *   *   *

MAN OF
HER DREAMS?

Will sexy Libra Jared Dalton make Kendall Arden's dreams come true? Find out in Patricia Ellis's PILLOW TALK, October's WRITTEN IN THE STARS book!

Kendall didn't know what she was letting herself in for when she agreed to help the perfect Libra with his psychology project. Jared's every glance awoke feelings she'd never before experienced—and promised to fulfill *all* her fantasies....

PILLOW TALK by Patricia Ellis ... only from Silhouette Romance in October. It's WRITTEN IN THE STARS!

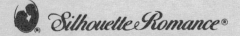

Silhouette Romance®

SILHOUETTE®
OFFICIAL SWEEPSTAKES RULES

NO PURCHASE NECESSARY

1. To enter, complete an Official Entry Form or 3"× 5" index card by hand-printing, in plain block letters, your complete name, address, phone number and age, and mailing it to: Silhouette Fashion A Whole New You Sweepstakes, P.O. Box 621, Fort Erie, Ontario L2A 5X3.

   No responsibility is assumed for lost, late or misdirected mail. Entries must be sent separately with first class postage affixed, and be received no later than December 31, 1991 for eligibility.

2. Winners will be selected by D.L. Blair, Inc., an independent judging organization whose decisions are final, in random drawings to be held on January 30, 1992 in Blair, NE at 10:00 a.m. from among all eligible entries received.

3. The prizes to be awarded and their approximate retail values are as follows: Grand Prize — A brand-new Ford Explorer 4×4 plus a trip for two (2) to Hawaii, including round-trip air transportation, six (6) nights hotel accommodation, a $1,400 meal/spending money stipend and $2,000 cash toward a new fashion wardrobe (approximate value: $28,000) or $15,000 cash; two (2) Second Prizes — A trip to Hawaii, including round-trip air transportation, six (6) nights hotel accommodation, a $1,400 meal/spending money stipend and $2,000 cash toward a new fashion wardrobe (approximate value: $11,000) or $5,000 cash; three (3) Third Prizes — $2,000 cash toward a new fashion wardrobe. All prizes are valued in U.S. currency. Travel award air transportation is from the commercial airport nearest winner's home. Travel is subject to space and accommodation availability, and must be completed by June 30, 1993. Sweepstakes offer is open to residents of the U.S. and Canada who are 21 years of age or older as of December 31, 1991, except residents of Puerto Rico, employees and immediate family members of Torstar Corp., its affiliates, subsidiaries, and all agencies, entities and persons connected with the use, marketing, or conduct of this sweepstakes. All federal, state, provincial, municipal and local laws apply. Offer void wherever prohibited by law. Taxes and/or duties, applicable registration and licensing fees, are the sole responsibility of the winners. Any litigation within the province of Quebec respecting the conduct and awarding of a prize may be submitted to the Régie des loteries et courses du Québec. All prizes will be awarded; winners will be notified by mail. No substitution of prizes is permitted.

4. Potential winners must sign and return any required Affidavit of Eligibility/Release of Liability within 30 days of notification. In the event of noncompliance within this time period, the prize may be awarded to an alternate winner. Any prize or prize notification returned as undeliverable may result in the awarding of that prize to an alternate winner. By acceptance of their prize, winners consent to use of their names, photographs or their likenesses for purposes of advertising, trade and promotion on behalf of Torstar Corp. without further compensation. Canadian winners must correctly answer a time-limited arithmetical question in order to be awarded a prize.

5. For a list of winners (available after 3/31/92), send a separate stamped, self-addressed envelope to: Silhouette Fashion A Whole New You Sweepstakes, P.O. Box 4665, Blair, NE 68009.

PREMIUM OFFER TERMS
To receive your gift, complete the Offer Certificate according to directions. Be certain to enclose the required number of "Fashion A Whole New You" proofs of product purchase (which are found on the last page of every specially marked "Fashion A Whole New You" Silhouette or Harlequin romance novel). Requests must be received no later than December 31, 1991. Limit: four (4) gifts per name, family, group, organization or address. Items depicted are for illustrative purposes only and may not be exactly as shown. Please allow 6 to 8 weeks for receipt of order. Offer good while quantities of gifts last. In the event an ordered gift is no longer available, you will receive a free, previously unpublished Silhouette or Harlequin book for every proof of purchase you have submitted with your request, plus a refund of the postage and handling charge you have incurred. Offer good in the U.S. and Canada only.

SLFC-SWPR

SILHOUETTE® OFFICIAL SWEEPSTAKES ENTRY FORM

4-FCSRS-1

Complete and return this Entry Form immediately – the more entries you submit, the better your chances of winning!

- Entries must be received by **December 31, 1991.**
- A Random draw will take place on **January 30, 1992.**
- No purchase necessary.

Yes, I want to win a FASHION A WHOLE NEW YOU Sensuous and Adventurous prize from Silhouette:

Name _____ Telephone _____ Age _____

Address _____

City _____ Province _____ Postal Code _____

Return Entries to: **Silhouette FASHION A WHOLE NEW YOU,**
P.O. Box 621, Fort Erie, Ontario L2A 5X3   © 1991 Harlequin Enterprises Limited

PREMIUM OFFER

To receive your free gift, send us the required number of proofs-of-purchase from any specially marked FASHION A WHOLE NEW YOU Silhouette or Harlequin Book with the Offer Certificate properly completed, plus a check or money order (do not send cash) to cover postage and handling payable to Silhouette FASHION A WHOLE NEW YOU Offer. We will send you the specified gift.

OFFER CERTIFICATE

Item	A. SENSUAL DESIGNER VANITY BOX COLLECTION (set of 4) (Suggested Retail Price $60.00)	B. ADVENTUROUS TRAVEL COSMETIC CASE SET (set of 3) (Suggested Retail Price $25.00)
# of proofs-of-purchase	18	12
Postage and Handling	$4.00	$3.45
Check one	☐	☐

Name _____

Address _____

City _____ Province _____ Postal Code _____

Mail this certificate, designated number of proofs-of-purchase and check or money order for postage and handling to: **Silhouette FASHION A WHOLE NEW YOU Gift Offer,** P.O. Box 622, Fort Erie, Ontario L2A 5X3. Requests must be received by December 31, 1991.

ONE PROOF-OF-PURCHASE

4-FWCSR-1

To collect your fabulous free gift you must include the necessary number of proofs-of-purchase with a properly completed Offer Certificate.

© 1991 Harlequin Enterprises Limited

See previous page for details.